the FAERY FLAG

STORIES AND POEMS OF FANTASY
AND THE SUPERNATURAL

JANE YOLEN

The FAERY FLAG

STORIES AND POEMS OF FANTASY AND THE SUPERNATURAL

ORCHARD BOOKS
A DIVISION OF FRANKLIN WATTS, INC.

NEW YORK

ACKNOWLEDGMENTS

Some of the stories and poems in this collection have appeared previously elsewhere. The Publisher herewith gratefully acknowledges permission received to include the following in this book: " 'Once Upon a Time . . .' She Said," from *National Storytelling Journal*; "The Foxwife," from the *World Fantasy Convention* program book, also appeared in *Moonsinger's Friends* (Bluejay Books); "Sir John Mandeville's Report on the Griffin," from *Isaac Asimov's Science Fiction Magazine*; "Wolf/Child," from *Twilight Zone Magazine*; "The Making of Dragons," from *Isaac Asimov's Science Fiction Magazine*; "The Tower Bird," from *Ariel Four*; "The Face in the Cloth," from *The Magazine of Fantasy and Science Fiction*; "Happy Dens; Or a Day in the Old Wolves' Home," from *Elsewhere, Vol. III* (Ace Fantasy Books); all these by permission of Curtis Brown Ltd. Also, "Words of Power," from *Visions* (Delacorte Books), by permission of Delacorte Books and Curtis Brown Ltd., and "The Boy Who Drew Unicorns," from *The Unicorn Treasury* (Doubleday), by permission of Doubleday and Curtis Brown Ltd.

Orchard Books
A division of Franklin Watts, Inc.
387 Park Avenue South, New York, NY 10016

The text of this book is set in 12 pt. Sabon
Manufactured in the United States of America
BOOK DESIGN BY SYLVIA FREZZOLINI

10   9   8   7   6   5   4   3   2

LIBRARY OF CONGRESS CATALOGING-IN-PUBLICATION DATA
Yolen, Jane.   The faery flag: stories and poems of fantasy and the supernatural [Jane Yolen]. p. cm. Summary: A collection of stories and poems on various fairy tale, ghost, or supernatural themes.
ISBN 0-531-05838-7.—ISBN 0-531-08438-8 (lib. bdg.)
1. Supernatural—Juvenile fiction. 2. Supernatural—Juvenile poetry. 3. Children's stories, American. 4. Children's poetry, American.
[1. Supernatural—Fiction. 2. Supernatural—Poetry. 3. Short stories. 4. American poetry.] I. Title.   88-34866
PZ7.Y78Fai   1989   CIP
[Fic]—dc19   AC

FOR THE MINNEAPOLIS FANTASY CREW:

Emma and Will

Pamela and D.B.

Kara

Pat

Mike

Lojo and Janie

Steve

but especially Adam and Betsy

CONTENTS

"ONCE UPON A TIME . . ."
SHE SAID

"Once upon a time," she said,
and the world began anew:
a vee of geese flew by,
plums roasting in their breasts;
a vacant-eyed princess
sat upon a hillock of glass;
a hut strolled through a wood
on chicken feet,
its toenails black and hard;
a horse's head proclaimed advice
from the impost of an arch;
one maiden spoke in toads,
another in pearls,
and a third with the nightingale's voice.
If you ask me,
I would have to say
all the world's magic
comes directly from the mouth.

1

THE FAERY FLAG

Long ago, when the wind blew from one corner of Skye to another without ever encountering a house higher than a tree, the faery folk lived on the land and they were called the *Daoine Sithe*, the Men of Peace. They loved the land well and shepherded its flocks, and never a building did they build that could not be dismantled in a single night or put up again in a single day.

But then human folk set foot upon the isles and scoured them with their rough shoeing. And before long both rock and tree were in the employ of men; the land filled with forts and houses, byres and pens. Boats plowed the seas and netted the fish. Stones were piled up for fences between neighbors.

The *Daoine Sithe* were not pleased, not pleased at all. An edict went out from the faery chief: *Have nothing to do with this humankind*.

And for year upon year it was so.

Now one day, the young laird of the MacLeod clan—Jamie was his name—walked out beyond his manor seeking a brachet hound lost outside in the night. It was his favorite hound, as old as he, which—since he was just past fifteen years—was quite old indeed.

He called its name. "Leoid. Leeeeeeoid." The wind sent back the name against his face but the dog never answered.

The day was chill, the wind was cold, and a white mist swirled about the young laird. But many days on Skye are thus, and he thought no more about the chill and cold than that he must find his old hound lest it die.

Jamie paid no heed to where his feet led him, through the bogs and over the hummocks. This was his land, after all, and he knew it well. He could not see the towering crags of the Black Cuillins, though he knew they were there. He could not hear the seals calling from the bay. Leoid was all he cared about. A MacLeod takes care of his own.

So without knowing it, he crossed over a strange, low, stone *drochit*, a bridge the likes of which he would never have found on a sunny day, for it was the bridge into Faerie.

No sooner had he crossed over than he heard his old dog barking. He would have known that sound were there a hundred howling hounds.

"Leoid!" he called. And the dog ran up to him, its hind end wagging, eager as a pup, so happy it was to see him. It had been made young again in the land of Faerie.

Jamie gathered the dog in his arms and was just turning to go home when he heard a girl calling from behind him.

"Leoid. Leoid." Her voice was as full of longing as his own had been just moments before.

He turned back, the dog still in his arms, and the fog lifted.

Running toward him was the most beautiful girl he had ever seen. Her dark hair was wild with curls, her black eyes wide, her mouth generous and smiling.

"Boy, you have found my dog. Give it me."

Now that was surely no way to speak to the young laird of the MacLeods, he who would someday be the chief. But the girl did not seem to know him. And surely he did not know the girl, though he knew everyone under his father's rule.

"This is my dog," said Jamie.

The girl came closer and put out her hand. She touched him on his bare arm. Where her hand touched, he felt such a shock, he thought he would die, but of love not of fear. Yet he did not.

"It is my dog now, Jamie MacLeod," she said. "It has crossed over the bridge. It has eaten the food of the *Daoine Sithe* and drunk our honey wine. If you bring it back to your world it will die at once and crumble into dust."

The young laird set the dog down and it frolicked about his feet. He put his hand into the girl's but was not shocked again.

"I will give it back to you for your name—and a kiss," he said.

"Be warned," answered the girl.

"I know about faery kisses," said Jamie, "but I am not afraid. And as you know my name, it is only fair that I should know yours."

"What we consider fair, you do not, young laird," she said. But she stood on tiptoe and kissed him on the brow. "Do not come back across the bridge, or you will break your parents' hearts."

He handed her the sprig of juniper from his bonnet.

She kissed the sprig as well and put it in her hair. "My name is Aizel and, like the red hot cinder, I burn what I touch." Then she whistled for the dog and they disappeared at once into the mist.

Jamie put his hand to his brow where Aizel had kissed him, and indeed she had burned him, it was still warm and sweet to his touch.

Despite the faery girl's warning, Jamie MacLeod looked for the bridge not once but many times. He left off fishing to search for it, and interrupted his hunting to search for it; and often he left his bed when the mist was thick to seek it. But even in the mist and the rain and the fog he could not find it. Yet he never stopped longing for the bridge to the girl.

His mother and father grew worried. They guessed by the mark on his brow what had occurred. So they gave great parties and threw magnificent balls that in this way the young laird might meet a human girl and forget the girl of the *Daoine Sithe*.

But never was there a girl he danced with that he danced with again. Never a girl he held that he held for long. Never a girl he kissed that he did not remember Aizel at the bridge. As time went on, his mother and father grew so desperate for him to give the MacLeods an heir, that they would have let him marry any young woman at all, even a faery maid.

On the eve of Jamie's twenty-first birthday, there was a great gathering of the clan at Dunvegan Castle. All the lights were set out along the castle wall and they twinned themselves down in the bay below.

Jamie walked the ramparts and stared out across the bogs and drums. "Oh Aizel," he said with a great sigh, "if I could but see you one more time. One more time and I'd be content."

And then he thought he heard the barking of a dog.

Now there were hounds in the castle and hounds in the town and hounds who ran every day under his horse's hooves. But he knew that particular call.

"Leoid!" he whispered to himself. He raced down the stairs and out the great doors with a torch in his hand, following the barking across the bog.

It was a misty, moisty evening, but he seemed to know the way. And he came quite soon to the cobbled bridge that he had so long sought. For a moment he hesitated, then went on.

There, in the middle, not looking a day older than when he had seen her six years before, stood Aizel in her green gown. Leoid was by her side.

"Into your majority, young laird," said Aizel. "I called to wish you the best."

"It is the best, now that I can see you," Jamie said. He smiled. "And my old dog."

Aizel smiled back. "No older than when last you saw us."

"I have thought of you every day since you kissed me," said Jamie. "And longed for you every night. Your brand still burns on my brow."

"I warned you of faery kisses," said Aizel.

He lifted his bonnet and pushed away his fair hair to show her the mark.

"I have thought of you, too, young laird," said Aizel. "And how the MacLeods have kept the peace in this unpeaceful land. My chief says I may bide with you for a while."

"How long a while?" asked Jamie.

"A faery while," replied Aizel. "A year or an heir, whichever comes first."

"A year is such a short time," Jamie said.

"I can make it be forever," Aizel answered.

With that riddle Jamie was content. And they walked back to Dunvegan Castle hand in hand, though they left the dog behind.

If Aizel seemed less fey in the starlight, Jamie did not mind. If he was only human, she did not seem to care. Nothing really mattered but his hand in hers, her hand in his, all the way back to his home.

The chief of the MacLeods was not pleased and his wife was not happy with the match. But that Jamie smiled and was content made them hold their tongues. So the young laird and the faery maid were married that night and bedded before day.

And in the evening Aizel came to them and said, "The MacLeods shall have their heir."

The days went fast and slow, warm and cold, and longer than a human it took for the faery girl to bear a child. But on the last day of the year she had lived with them, Aizel was brought to labor till with a great happy sigh she birthed a beautiful babe.

"A boy!" the midwife cried out, standing on a chair and showing the child so that all the MacLeods might see.

A great cheer ran around the castle then. "An heir. An heir to the MacLeods!"

Jamie was happy for that, but happier still that his faery wife was well. He bent to kiss her brow.

"A year or an heir, that was all I could promise. But I have given you forever," she said. "The MacLeods shall prosper and Dunvegan will never fall."

Before he could say a word in return, she had vanished and the bed was bare, though her outline could be seen on the linens for a moment more.

The cheer was still echoing along the stone passageways as the midwife carried the babe from room to room to show him to all the clan. But the young laird of the MacLeods put his head in his hands and wept.

Later that night, when the fires were high in every hearth and blaeberry wine filled every cup; when the harp and fiddle rang throughout Dunvegan with their tunes; when the bards' mouths swilled with whisky and swelled with the old songs; and even the nurse was dancing with her man, the young laird Jamie MacLeod walked the castle ramparts seven times round, mourning for his lost faery wife.

The youngest laird of the MacLeods lay in his cradle all alone.

So great was the celebration that no one was watching him. And in the deepest part of the night, he kicked off his blankets as babies often do, and he cried out with the cold.

But no one came to cover him. Not the nurse dancing with her man, nor his grandam listening to the tunes, nor his grandfather drinking with his men, nor his father on the castle walk. No one heard the poor wee babe crying with the cold.

It was a tiny cry, a thin bit of sound threaded out into the dark. It went over hillock and hill, over barrow and bog, crossed the cobbled *drochit*, and wound its way into Faerie itself.

Now they were celebrating in the faery world as well, not for the birth of the child but for the return of their own. There was feasting and dancing and the singing of tunes. There was honey wine and faery pipes and the high, sweet laughter of the *Daoine Sithe*.

But in all that fine company, Aizel alone did not sing and dance. She sat in her great chair with her arms around her brachet hound. If there were tears in her eyes, you would not have known it, for the *Daoine Sithe* do not cry, and besides the hound had licked away every one. But she heard that tiny sound as any mother would. Distracted, she stood.

"What is it, my daughter?" asked the great chief of the *Daoine Sithe* when he saw her stand, when he saw a single tear that Leoid had not had time to lick away.

But before any of the fey could tell her no, Aizel ran from the faery hall, the dog at her heels. She raced across the bridge, herself as insubstantial as the mist. And behind her came the faery troops. And the dog.

The company of fey stopped at the edge of the bridge and watched Aizel go. Leoid followed right after. But no sooner had the dog's legs touched the earth on the other side than it crumbled into dust.

Aizel hesitated not a moment, but followed that thread of sound, winding her back into the world of men. She walked over bog and barrow, over hill and hillock, through the great wooden doors and up the castle stairs.

When she entered the baby's room, he was between one breath and another.

"There, there," Aizel said, leaning over the cradle and covering him with her shawl, "thy Mama's here." She rocked him till he fell back asleep, warm and content. Then she kissed him on the brow, leaving a tiny mark there for all to see, and vanished in the morning light.

The nurse found the babe sleeping soundly well into the day. He was wrapped in a cloth of stranger's weave. His thumb was in his mouth, along with a piece of the shawl. She did not know how the cloth got there, nor did his grandfather, the Great MacLeod. If his grandmother guessed, she did not say.

But the young laird Jamie knew. He knew that Aizel had been drawn back across the bridge by her son's crying, as surely as he had first been led to her by the barking of his hound.

"Love calls to love," he whispered softly to his infant son as he held him close. "And the fey, like the MacLeods take care of their own."

The faery shawl still hangs on the wall at Dunvegan Castle on the Isle of Skye. Only now it is called a Faery Flag and the MacLeods carry it foremost into battle. I have seen it there. Like this story, it is a tattered remnant of stranger's weave and as true and warming as you let it be.

THE FOXWIFE

It was the spring of the year. Blossoms sat like painted butterflies on every tree. But the student Jiro did not enjoy the beauty. He was angry. It seemed he was always angry at something. And he was especially angry because he had just been told by his teachers that the other students feared him and his rages.

"You must go to a far island," said the master of his school.

"Why?" asked Jiro angrily.

"I will tell you if you listen," said his master with great patience.

Jiro shut his mouth and ground his teeth but was otherwise silent.

"You must go to the furthest island you can find. An island where no other person lives. There you must study by yourself. And in the silence of your own heart you may yet find the peace you need."

Raging, Jiro packed his tatami mat, his book, and his brushes. He put them in a basket and tied the basket to his back. Though he was angry—with his master and with all the teachers and

12

students in his school—he really *did* want to learn how to remain calm. And so he set out.

Sometimes he crossed bridges. Sometimes he waded rivers. Sometimes he took boats across the wild water. But at last he came to a small island where, the boatman assured him, no other person lived.

"Come once a week and bring me supplies," said Jiro, handing the boatman a coin. Then Jiro went inland and walked through the sparse woods until he came to a clearing in which he found a deserted temple.

"Odd," thought Jiro. "The boatman did not mention such a thing." He walked up the temple steps and was surprised to find the temple clean. He set his basket down in one corner, pulled out his mat, and spread it on the floor.

"This will be my home," he said. He said it out loud and there was an edge still to his voice.

For many days Jiro stayed on the island, working from first light till last. And though once in a while he became angry—because his brush would not write properly or because a dark cloud dared to hide the sun—for the most part he was content.

One day, when Jiro was in the middle of a particularly complicated text and having much trouble with it, he looked up and saw a girl walking across the clearing toward him.

Every few steps she paused and glanced around. She was not frightened but rather seemed alert, as if ready for flight.

Jiro stood up. "Go away," he called out, waving his arm.

The girl stopped. She put her head to one side as if considering him. Then she continued walking as before.

Jiro did not know what to do. He wondered if she were the

13

boatman's daughter. Perhaps she had not heard him. Perhaps she was stupid. Perhaps she was deaf. She certainly did not belong on *his* island. He called out louder this time, "Go away. I am a student and must not be disturbed." He followed each statement with a movement of his arms.

But the girl did not go away and she did not stop. In fact, at his voice, she picked up her skirts and came toward him at a run.

Jiro was amazed. She ran faster than anyone he had ever seen, her dark russet hair streaming out behind her like a tail. In a moment she was at the steps of the temple.

"Go away!" cried Jiro for the third time.

The girl stopped, stared, and bowed.

Politeness demanded that Jiro return her bow. When he looked up again, she was gone.

Satisfied, Jiro smiled and turned back to his work. But there was the girl, standing stone-still by his scrolls and brushes, her hands folded before her.

"I am Kitsune," she said. "I care for the temple."

Jiro could contain his anger no longer. "Go away," he screamed. "I must work alone. I came to this island because I was assured no other person lived here."

She stood as still as a stone in a river and let the waves of his rage break against her. Then she spoke. "No other person lives here. I am Kitsune. I care for the temple."

After that, storm as he might, there was nothing Jiro could do. The girl simply would not go away.

She did care for the temple—and Jiro as well. Once a week she appeared and swept the floors. She kept a bowl filled with fresh camellias by his bed. And once, when he had gone to get his supplies and tripped and hurt his legs, Kitsune found him and carried him to the temple on her back. After that, she came every day, as if aware Jiro needed constant attention. Yet she never spoke unless he spoke first, and even then her words were few.

Jiro wondered at her. She was little, lithe, and light. She moved with a peculiar grace. Every once in a while, he would see her stop and put her head to one side in that attitude of listening. He never heard what it was she heard, and he never dared ask.

At night she disappeared. One moment she would be there and the next moment gone. But in the morning Jiro would wake to find her curled in sleep at his feet. She would not say where she had been.

So spring passed, and summer, too. Jiro worked well in the quiet world Kitsune helped him maintain, and he found a kind of peace beginning to bud in his heart.

On the first day of fall, with leaves being shaken from the trees by the wind, Jiro looked up from his books. He saw that Kitsune sat on the steps trembling.

"What is it?" he asked.

"The leaves. Aieee, the leaves," she cried. Then she jumped up and ran down to the trees. She leapt and played with the leaves as they fell about her. They caught in her hair. She blew them off her face. She rolled in them. She put her face to the ground and sniffed the dirt. Then, as if a fever had suddenly left her, she was still. She stood up, brushed off her clothing, smoothed her hair, and came back to sit quietly on the steps again.

Jiro was enchanted. He had never seen any woman like this before. He left his work and sat down on the steps beside her. Taking her hand in his, he stroked it thoughtfully, then

15

brought it slowly to his cheek. Her hand was warm and dry.

"We must be married," he said at last. "I would have you with me always."

"Always? What is always?" asked Kitsune. She tried to pull away.

Jiro held her hand tightly and would not let her go. And after a while she agreed.

The boatman took them across to the mainland, where they found a priest who married them at once, though he smiled behind his hand at their haste. Jiro was supremely happy and he knew that Kitsune must be, too, though all the way in the boat going there and back again, she shuddered and would not look out across the waves.

That night Kitsune shared the tatami mat with Jiro. When the moon was full and the night whispered softly about the temple, Jiro awoke. He turned to look at Kitsune, his bride. She was not there.

"Kitsune," he called out fearfully. He sat up and looked around. He could not see her anywhere. He got up and searched around the temple, but she was not to be found. At last he fell asleep, sitting on the temple steps. When he awoke again at dawn, Kitsune was curled in sleep on the mat.

"Where were you last night?" he demanded.

"Where I should be," she said and would say no more.

Jiro felt anger flowering inside, so he turned sharply from her and went to his books. But he did not try to calm himself. He fed his rage silently. All day he refused to speak. At night, exhausted by his own anger, he fell asleep before dark. He woke at midnight to find Kitsune gone.

Jiro knew he had to stay awake until she returned. A little before dawn he saw her running across the clearing. She ran up the temple steps and did not seem to be out of breath. She came right to the mat, surprised to see Jiro awake.

Jiro waited for her explanation, but instead of speaking she began her morning chores. She had fresh camellias in her hands, which she put in a bowl as if nothing were wrong.

Jiro sat up. "Where do you go at night?" he asked. "What do you do?"

Kitsune did not answer.

Jiro leaped up and came over to her. He took her by the shoulders and began to shake her. "Where? Where do you go?" he cried.

Kitsune dropped the bowl of flowers and it shattered. The water spread out in little islands of puddles on the floor. She looked down and her hair fell around her shoulders, hiding her face.

Jiro could not look at the trembling figure so obviously terrified of him. Instead, he bent to pick up the pieces of the bowl. He saw his own face mirrored a hundred times in the spilled drops. Then he saw something else. Instead of Kitsune's face or her russet hair, he saw the sharp-featured head of a fox reflected there. The fox's little pointed ears were twitching. Out of its dark eyes tears began to fall.

Jiro looked up but there was no fox. Only Kitsune, beginning to weep, trembling at the sight of him, unable to move. And then he knew. She was a *nogitsone*, a were-fox, who could take the shape of a beautiful woman. But the *nogitsone*'s reflection in the water was always that of a beast.

Suddenly Jiro's anger, fueled by his terror, knew no bounds.

"You are not human," he cried. "Monster, wild thing, demon, beast. You will rip me or tear me if I let you stay. Some night you will gnaw upon my bones. Go away."

As he spoke, Kitsune fell to her hands and knees. She shook herself once, then twice. Her hair seemed to flow over her body, covering her completely. Then twitching her ears once, the vixen raced down the temple steps, across the meadow, and out of sight.

Jiro stood and watched for a long, long time. He thought he could see the red flag of her tail many hours after she had gone.

The snows came early that year, but the season was no colder than Jiro's heart. Every day he thought he heard the barking of a fox in the woods beyond the meadow, but he would not call it in. Instead he stood on the steps and cried out, "Away. Go away." At night he dreamed of a woman weeping close by his mat. In his sleep he called out, "Away. Go away."

Then when winter was full and the nights bitter cold, the sounds ceased. The island was deadly still. In his heart Jiro knew the fox was gone for good. Even his anger was gone, guttered in the cold like a candle. What had seemed so certain to him, in the heat of his rage, was certain no more. He wondered over and over which had been human and which had been beast. He even composed a haiku on it.

> *Pointed ears, red tail,*
> *Wife covered in fox's skin,*
> *The beast hides within.*

He said it over many times to himself but was never satisfied with it.

18

Spring came suddenly, a tiny green blade pushing through the snow. And with it came a strange new sound. Jiro woke to it, out of a dream of snow. He followed the sound to the temple steps and saw prints in the dust of white. Sometimes they were fox, sometimes girl, as if the creature who made them could not make up its mind.

"Kitsune," Jiro called out impulsively. Perhaps she had not died after all.

He looked out across the meadow and thought he saw again that flag of red. But the sound that had wakened him came once more, from behind. He turned, hoping to see Kitsune standing again by the mat with the bowl of camellias in her hands. Instead, by his books, he saw a tiny bundle of russet fur. He went over and knelt by it. Huddled together for warmth were two tiny kit foxes.

For a moment Jiro could feel the anger starting inside him. He did not want these two helpless, mewling things. He wanted Kitsune. Then he remembered that he had driven her away. Away. And the memory of that long, cold winter without her put out the budding flames of his new rage.

He reached out and put his hands on the foxlings. At his touch, they sprang apart on wobbly legs, staring up at him with dark, discerning eyes. They trembled so, he was afraid they might fall.

"There, there," he crooned to them. "This big, rough beast will not hurt you. Come. Come to me." He let them sniff both his hands, and when their trembling ceased, he picked them up and cradled them against his body, letting them share his warmth. First one, then the other, licked his fingers. This so moved Jiro that, without meaning to, he began to cry.

19

The tears dropped onto the muzzles of the foxlings and they looked as if they, too, were weeping. Then, as Jiro watched, the kits began to change. The features of a human child slowly superimposed themselves on each fox face. Sighing, they snuggled closer to Jiro, closed their eyes, put their thumbs in their mouths, and slept.

Jiro smiled. Walking very carefully, as if afraid each step might jar the babies awake, he went down the temple steps. He walked across the clearing leaving man-prints in the unmarked snow. Slowly, calmly, all anger gone from him, he moved toward the woods where he knew Kitsune waited. He would find her before evening came again.

WORDS OF POWER

Late Blossoming Flower, the only child of her mother's old age, stared sulkily into the fire. A homely child, with a nose that threatened to turn into a beak and a mouth that seldom smiled, she was nonetheless cherished by her mother and the clan. Her loneness, the striking rise of her nose, the five strands of white hair that streaked through her shiny black hair, were all seen as the early signs of great power, the power her mother had given up when she had chosen to bear a child.

"I would never have made such a choice," Late Blossoming Flower told her mother. "I would never give up *my* power."

Her mother, who had the same fierce nose, the streak of white hair and bitter smile, but was a striking beauty, replied gently, "You do not have that power yet. And if I had not given up mine, you would not be here now to make such a statement and to chide me for my choice." She shook her head. "Nor would you now be scolded for forgetting to do those things which are yours by duty."

Late Blossoming Flower bit back the reply that was no reply but merely angry words. She rose from the fireside and went out of the cliff-house to feed the milk-beast. As she climbed down the withy ladder to the valley below, she rehearsed that conversation with her mother as she had done so often before. Always her mother remained calm, her voice never rising into anger. It infuriated Flower and she nursed that sore like all the others, counting them up as carefully as if she were toting them on a notch-stick. The tally by now was long indeed.

But soon, she reminded herself, soon she would herself be a woman of power though she was late coming to it. All the signs but one were on her. Under the chamois shirt her breasts had finally begun to bud. There was hair curling in the secret places of her body. Her waist and hips were changing to create a place for the Herb Belt to sit comfortably, instead of chafing her as it did now. And when finally the moon called to her and her first blood flowed, cleansing her body of man's sin, she would be allowed at last to go on her search for her own word of power and be free of her hated, ordinary chores. Boys could not go on such a search for they were never able to rid themselves of the dirty blood-sin. But she took no great comfort in that, for not all girls who sought found. Still, Late Blossoming Flower knew she was the daughter of a woman of power, a woman so blessed that even though she had had a child and lost the use of the Shaping Hands she still retained the Word That Changes. Late Blossoming Flower never doubted that when she went on her journey she would find what it was she sought.

The unfed milk-beast lowed longingly as her feet touched the ground. She bent and gathered up bits of earth, cupped the frag-

ments in her hand, said the few phrases of the *Ke-waha*, the prayer
to the land, then stood.

"I'm not *that* late," she said sharply to the agitated beast, and
went to the wooden manger for maize.

It was the first day after the rising of the second moon and the
florets of the night-blooming panomom tree were open wide. The
sickly sweet smell of the tiny clustered blossoms filled the valley,
and all the women of the valley dreamed dreams.

The women of power dreamed in levels. Late Blossoming Flower's mother passed from one level to another with the ease of long
practice but her daughter's dream quester had difficulty going
through. She wandered too long on the dreamscape paths searching for a ladder or a rope or some other familiar token of passage.

When Late Blossoming Flower had awakened, her mother
scolded her for her restless sleep.

"If you are to be a true woman of power, you must force
yourself to lie down in the dream and fall asleep. Sleep within
sleep, dream within dream. Only then will you wake at the next
level." Her head had nodded gently every few words and she
spoke softly, braiding her hair with quick and supple hands. "You
must be like a gardener forcing an early bud to bring out the
precious juices."

"Words. Just words," said Late Blossoming Flower. "And none
of *those* words has power." She had risen from her pallet, shaking
her own hair free of the loose night braiding, brushing it fiercely
before plaiting it up again. She could not bear to listen to her
mother's advice any longer, and had let her thoughts drift instead
to the reed hut on the edge of the valley where old Sand Walker

23

lived. A renegade healer, he lived apart from the others and, as a man, was little thought of. But Late Blossoming Flower liked to go and sit with him and listen to his stories of the time before time when power had been so active in the world it could be plucked out of the air as easily as fruit from a tree. He said that dreams eventually explained themselves and that to discipline the dream figure was to bind its power. To Late Blossoming Flower that made more sense than all her mother's constant harping on the Forcing Way.

So intent was she on visiting the old man that day, she had raced through her chores, scanting the milk-beast and the birds who squatted on hidden nests. She had collected only a few eggs and left them in the basket at the bottom of the cliff. Then, without a backward glance at the withy ladders spanning the levels or the people moving busily against the cliff face, she raced down the path toward Sand Walker's home.

As a girl child she had that freedom, given leave for part of each day to walk the many trails through the valley. On these walks she was supposed to learn the ways of the growing flowers, to watch the gentler creatures at their play, to come to a careful understanding of the way of predator and prey. It was time for her to know the outer landscape of her world as thoroughly as she would, one day, know the inner dream trails. But Late Blossoming Flower was a hurrying child. As if to make up for her late birth and the crushing burden of early power laid on her, she refused to take the time.

"My daughter," her mother often cautioned her, "a woman of true power must be in love with silence. You must learn to ignore all the outward sounds in order to approach the silence that lies within."

But Flower wanted no inner silence. She delighted in tuneless singing and loud sounds: the sharp hoarse cry of the night herons sailing across the marsh; the crisp howl of the jackals calling under the moon; even the scream of the rabbit in the teeth of the wolf. She sought to imitate *those* sounds, make them louder, sing them again in her own mouth. What was silence compared to sound?

And when she was with old Sand Walker in his hut, he sang with her. And told stories, joking stories, about the old women and their silences.

"Soon enough," Sand Walker said, "soon enough it will be silent and dark. In the grave. Those old *bawenahs* . . ." and he used the word that meant the unclean female vulture, "those old *bawenahs* would make us rehearse for our coming deaths with their binding dreams. Laugh *now*, child. Sing out. Silence is for the dead ones, though they call themselves alive and walk the trails. But you and I, ho . . ." and he poked her in the stomach lightly with his stick, ". . . we know the value of noise. It blocks out thinking and thinking means pain. Cry out for me, child. Loud. Louder."

And as if a trained dog, Late Blossoming Flower always dropped to her knees at this request and howled, scratching at the dirt, and wagging her bottom. Then she would fall over on her back with laughter and the old man laughed with her.

All this was in her mind as she ran along the path toward Sand Walker's hut.

A rabbit darted into her way, then zagged back to escape her pounding feet. A few branches, emboldened by the coming summer, strayed across her path and whipped her arm, leaving red scratches. Impatient with the marks, she ignored them.

At the final turning, the old man's hut loomed up. He was sitting in the doorway, as always, humming, and eating a piece of yellowed fruit, the juices running down his chin. At the noise of her coming he looked up and grinned.

"Hai!" he said, more sound than greeting.

Flower skidded to a stop and squatted in the dirt beside him.

"You look tired," he said. "Did you dream?"

"I tried. But dreaming is so slow," Flower admitted.

"Dreaming is not living. You and I—we live. Have a bite?" He offered her what was left of the fruit, mostly core.

She took it so as not to offend him, holding the core near her mouth but not eating. The smell of the overripe, sickly sweet fruit made her close her eyes and she was startled into a dream.

The fruit was in her mouth and she could feel its sliding passage down her throat. It followed the twists of her inner pathways, dropping seeds as it went, until it landed heavily in her belly. There it began to burn, a small but significant fire in her gut.

Bending over to ease the cramping, Flower turned her back on the old man's hut and crept along the trail toward the village. The trees along the trail and the muddle of gray-green wild flowers blurred into an indistinct mass as she went as if she were seeing them through tears, though her cheeks were dry and her eyes clear.

When she reached the cliffside she saw, to her surprise, that

26

the withy ladders went down into a great hole in the earth instead of up toward the dwellings on the cliff face.

It was deathly silent all around her. The usual chatter of children at their chores, the chant of women, the hum-buzz of men in the furrowed fields was gone. The cliff was as blank and smooth as the shells of the eggs she had gathered that morning.

And then she heard a low sound, compounded of moans and a strange hollow whistling, like an old man's laughter breathed out across a reed. Turning around she followed the sound. It led her to the hole. She bent over it and as she did the sound resolved itself into a single word: bawenah. *She saw a pale, shining face looking up at her from the hole, its mouth a smear of fruit. When the mouth opened, it was as round and as black as the hole. There were no teeth. There was no tongue. Yet still the mouth spoke:* bawenah.

Flower awoke and stared at the old man. Pulpy fruit stained his scraggly beard. His eyes were filmy. Slowly his tongue emerged and licked his lips.

She turned and without another word to him walked home. Her hands cupped her stomach, pressing and releasing, all the way back as if pressure alone could drive away the cramps.

Her mother was waiting for her at the top of the ladder, hands folded on her own belly. "So," she said, "it is your woman time."

Flower did not ask how she knew. Her mother was a woman of great power still and such knowledge was well within her grasp, though it annoyed Flower that it should be so.

"Yes," Flower answered, letting a small whine creep into

her voice. "But you did not tell me that it would hurt so."

"With some," her mother said, smiling and smoothing back the white stripe of hair with her hand, "with some womanhood comes easy. With some it comes harder." Then, as they walked into their rooms, she added with a bitterness uncharacteristic of her, "Could your *healer* not do something for you?"

Flower was startled that her mother was hurt by the association with the old man rather than merely annoyed. She began to answer, then bit back her first angry reply. Instead, mastering her voice, she said, "I did not think to ask him for help. He is but a man. *I* am a woman."

"You are a woman today, truly," her mother said. She went over to the great chest she had carved before Flower's birth, a chest made of the wood of a lightning-struck panomom tree. The chest's sides were covered with carved signs of power: the florets of the tree with their threefoil flowers, the mouse and hare who were her mother's personal signs, the trailing arbet vine which was her father's, and the signs for the four moons: quarter, half, full, and closed faces.

When she opened the chest it made a small creaking protest. Flower came over to look in. There, below her first cradle dress and leggings, nestled beside a tress of her first, fine baby hair, was the Herb Belt she had helped her mother make. It had fifteen pockets, one for each year she had been a girl.

They went outside and her mother raised her voice in the wild ululation that could call all the women of power to her. It echoed around the clearing and across the fields to the gathering streams beyond, a high, fierce yodeling. And then she called out again, this time in a gentler voice that would bring the women who had borne and their girl children with them.

28

Flower knew it would be at least an hour before they all gathered and in the meantime she and her mother had much to do.

They went back into the rooms and turned around all of the objects they owned as a sign that Flower's life would now be turned around as well. Bowls, cups, pitchers were turned. Baskets of food and the drying racks were turned. Even the heavy chest was turned around. They left the bed pallets to the very last and then, each holding an end, they walked the beds around until the ritual was complete.

Flower stripped in front of her mother, something she had not done completely in years. She resisted the impulse to cover her breasts. On her leggings was the blood sign. Carefully her mother packed those leggings into the panomom chest. Flower would not wear them again.

At the bottom of the chest, wrapped in a sweet-smelling woven grass covering were a white chamois dress and leggings. Flower's mother took them out and spread them on the bedding, her hand smoothing the nap. Then, with a pitcher of water freshened with violet flowers, she began to wash her daughter's body, using a scrub made of the leaves of the sandarac tree. The nubby sandarac and the soothing rinse of the violet water were to remind Flower of the fierce and gentle sides of womanhood. All the while she scrubbed, Flower's mother chanted the songs of Woman: the seven-fold chant of Rising, the Way of Power, and the Praise to Earth and Moon.

The songs reminded Flower of something, and she tried to think of what it was as her mother's hands cleansed her of the sins of youth. It was while her mother was braiding her hair, plaiting in it reed ribbons that ended in a dangle of shells, that Flower remembered. The chants were like the cradle songs her mother had sung her when she was a child, with the same rise and fall, the same liquid sounds. She suddenly wanted to cry for the loss of those times and the pain she had given her mother, and she wondered why she felt so like weeping when anger was her usual way.

The white dress and leggings slipped on easily, indeed fit her perfectly though she had never tried them on before and that, too, was a sign of her mother's power.

And what of her own coming power? Flower wondered as she stood in the doorway watching the women assemble at the foot of the ladder. The women of power stood in the front, then the birth women, last of all the girls. She could name them all, her friends, her sisters in the tribe, who only lately had avoided her because of her association with the old man. She tried to smile at them, but her mouth would not obey her. In fact, her lower lip trembled and she willed it to stop, finally clamping it with her teeth.

"She is a woman," Flower's mother called down to them, the ritual words. They had known, even without her statement, had known from that first wild cry, what had happened. "Today she has come into her power, putting it on as a woman dons her white dress, but she does not yet know her own way. She goes now, as we all go at our time, to the far hills and beyond to seek the Word That Changes. She may find it or not, but she will tell of that when she has returned."

The women below began to sway and chant the words of the Searching Song, words which Flower had sung with them for fifteen years without really understanding their meaning. Fifteen years—far longer than any of the other girls—standing at the ladder's foot and watching another Girl-Become-Woman go off on her search. And that was, she saw it now, why she had fallen under Sand Walker's spell.

But now, standing above the singers, waiting for the Belt and the Blessing, she felt for the first time how strongly the power called to her. This was *her* moment, *her* time, and there would be no other. She pictured the old man in his hut and realized that if she did not find her word she would be bound to him forever.

"Mother," she began, wondering if it were too late to say all the things she should have said before, but her mother was coming toward her with the Belt and suddenly it *was* too late. Once the Belt was around her waist, she could not speak again until the Word formed in her mouth, with or without its accompanying power. Tears started in her eyes.

Her mother saw the tears and perhaps she mistook them for something else. Tenderly she placed the Belt around Flower's waist, setting it on the hips, and tying it firmly behind her. Then she turned her daughter around, the way every object in the house had been turned, till she faced the valley again where all the assembled women could read the fear on her face.

> *"Into the valley, in the fear we all face,*
> *Into the morning of your womanhood,*
> *Go with our blessing to guide you,*
> *Go with our blessing to guard you,*
> *Go with our blessing and bring back your word."*

The chant finished, Flower's mother pushed her toward the ladder and went back into the room and sat on the chest to do her own weeping.

31

Flower opened her eyes, surprised, for she had not realized that she had closed them. All the women had disappeared, back into the fields, into the woods; she did not know where nor was she to wonder about them. Her journey had to be made alone. Talking to anyone who might query her on the road this day would spell an end to them both, to her own quest for her power, to the questioner's very life.

As she walked out of the village, Flower noticed that everything along the way seemed different. Her power had, indeed, begun. Each of the low bushes had a shadow self, like the moon's halo, standing behind. The trees were filled with eyes, peering out of the knotholes. The chattering of animals in the brush was a series of messages, though Flower knew that she was still unable to decipher them. And the path itself sparkled as if water rushed over it, tumbling the small stones.

She seemed to slip in and out of quick dreams that were familiar pieces of her old dreams stitched together in odd ways. Her childhood was sloughing off behind her with each step, a skin removed.

Further down the path, where the valley met the foothills leading to the far mountains, she could see Sand Walker's hut casting a long, dark, toothy shadow across the trail. Flower was not sure if the shadows lengthened because the sun was at the end of its day or if this was yet another dream. She closed her eyes and, when she opened them again, the long shadows were still there though not nearly as dark or as menacing.

When she neared the hut, the old man was sitting silently out front. His shadow, unlike the hut's black shadow, was a strange shade of green.

She did not dare greet the old man, for fear of ruining her quest and because she did not want to hurt him. One part of her was still here with him, wild, casting green shadows, awake. He had no protection against her power. But surely she might give him one small sign of recognition. Composing her hands in front of her, she was prepared to signal him with a finger, when without warning he leaped up, grinning.

"*Ma-hane*, white girl," he cried, jumping into her path. "Do not forget to laugh, you in your white dress and leggings. If you do not laugh, you are one of the dead ones."

In great fear she reached out a hand toward him to silence him before he could harm them both, and power sprang unbidden from her fingertips. She had forgotten the Shaping Hands. And though they were as yet untrained and untried, still they were a great power. She watched in horror as five separate arrows of flame struck the old man's face, touching his eyes, his nostrils, his mouth, sealing them, melting his features like candle wax. He began to shrink under the fire, growing smaller and smaller, fading into a gray-green splotch that only slowly resolved itself into the form of a *sa-hawa*, a butterfly the color of leaf mold.

Flower did not dare speak, not even a word of comfort. She reached down and shook out his crumpled shirt, loosing the butterfly. It flapped its wings, tentatively at first, then with more strength, and finally managed to flutter up toward the top of the hut.

Folding the old man's tattered shirt and leggings with gentle hands, Flower placed them carefully on the doorstep of his hut, still watching the fluttering *sa-hawa*. When she stood again, she had to shade her eyes with one hand to see it. It had flown away

33

from the hut and was hovering between patches of wild onion in a small meadow on the flank of the nearest foothill.

Flower bit her lip. How could she follow the butterfly? It was going up the mountainside and her way lay straight down the road. Yet how could she not follow it? Sand Walker's transformation had been her own doing. No one else could undo what she had so unthinkingly created.

To get to the meadow was easy. But if the butterfly went farther up the mountainside, what could she do? There was only a goat track and then the sheer cliff wall. As she hesitated, the *sa-hawa* rose into the air again, leaving the deep green spikes of onions, to fly up toward the mountain itself.

Flower looked quickly down the trail, but the shadows of oncoming evening had closed that way. Ahead, the Path of Power— her Power—was still brightly lit.

"Oh, Mother," she thought. "Oh, my mothers, I need your blessing indeed." And so thinking, she plunged into the underbrush after the *sa-hawa*, heedless of the thorns tugging at her white leggings or the light on the Path of Power that suddenly and inexplicably went out.

The goat path had not been used for years, not by goats or by humans either. Briars tangled across it. Little rock slides blocked many turnings and in others the pebbly surface slid away beneath her feet. Time and again she slipped and fell; her knees and palms bruised, and all the power in her Shaping Hands seemed to do no good. She could not call on it. Once when she fell she bit her underlip so hard it bled. And always, like some spirit guide, the little gray-green butterfly fluttered ahead, its wings glowing with five spots as round and marked as fingerprints.

Still Flower followed, unable to call out or cry out because a new woman on her quest for her Power must not speak until she has found her word. She still hoped, a doomed and forlorn hope, that once she had caught the *sa-hawa* she might also catch her Power or at least be allowed to continue on her quest. And she would take the butterfly with her and find at least enough of the Shaping Hands to turn him back into his own tattered, laughing, dismal self.

She went on. The only light now came from the five spots on the butterfly's wings and the pale moon rising over the jagged crest of First Mother, the leftmost mountain. The goat track had disappeared entirely. It was then the butterfly began to rise straight up, as if climbing the cliff face.

Out of breath, Flower stopped and listened first to her own ragged breathing, then to the pounding of her heart. At last she was able to be quiet enough to hear the sounds of the night. The butterfly stopped, too, as if it were listening as well.

From far down the valley she heard the rise and fall of the running dogs, howling at the moon, little chirrups of frogs, the pick-buzz of insect wings, and then the choughing of a nightbird's wings. She turned her head for a moment, fearful that it might be an eater-of-bugs. When she looked back, the *sa-hawa* was almost gone, edging up the great towering mountain that loomed over her.

Flower almost cried out then, in frustration and anger and fear, but she held her tongue and looked for a place to start the climb. She had to use hands and feet instead of eyes, for the moonlight made this a place of shadows, shadows within shadows, and only her hands and feet could see between the dark and dark.

She felt as if she had been climbing for hours, though the moon above her spoke of a shorter time, when the butterfly suddenly disappeared. Without the lure of its phosphorescent wings, Flower was too exhausted to continue. All the tears she had held back for so long suddenly rose to swamp her eyes. She snuffled loudly and crouched uncertainly on a ledge. Then huddling against the rockface she tried to stay awake, to draw warmth and courage from the mountain. But without wanting to, she fell asleep.

In the dream she spiraled up and up and up into the sky without ladder or rope to pull her, and she felt the words of a high scream fall from her lips, a yelping *kya*. She awoke terrified and shaking in the morning light, sitting on a thin ledge nearly a hundred feet up the mountainside. She had no memory of the climb and certainly saw no way to get down.

And then she saw the *sa-hawa* next to her and memory flooded back. She cupped her hand, ready to pounce on the butterfly when it fluttered its wings in the sunlight and moved from its perch. Desperate to catch it, she leaned out, lost her balance, and began to fall.

"Oh, Mother," she screamed in her mind, and a single word came back to her. *Aki-la*. Eagle. She screamed it aloud. "Aki-la!"

As she fell the bones of her arms lengthened and flattened, cracking sinew and marrow. Her small, sharp nose bone arched outward and she watched it slowly form into a black beak with a dull yellow membrane at the base. Her body, twisting, seemed to stretch, catching the wind, first beneath, then above; she could feel the swift air through her feathers and the high, sweet whistling of it rushing past her head. Spiraling up, she pumped her powerful wings once. Then, holding them flat, she soared.

36

Aki-la. Golden eagle, she thought. It was her Word of Power, the Word That Changes, hers and no one else's. And then all words left her and she knew only wind and sky and the land spread out far below.

How long she coursed the sky in her flat-winged glide she did not know. For her there was no time, no ticking off of moment after moment, only the long sweet soaring. But at last her stomach marked the time for her and, without realizing it, she was scanning the ground for prey. It was as if she had two sights now, one the sweeping farsight that showed her the land as a series of patterns, and the other that closed up the space whenever she saw movement or heat in the grass that meant some small creature was moving below.

At the base of the mountain she spied a large mouse and her wings knew even before her mind, even before her stomach. They cleaved to her side and she dove down in one long, perilous stoop toward the brown creature that was suddenly still in the short grass.

The wind rushed by her as she dove, and a high singing filled her head, wordless visions of meat and blood.

"Kya," she called, and followed it with a whistle. *"Kya,"* her hunting song.

Right before reaching the mouse, she threw out her wings and backwinged, extending her great claws as brakes. But her final sight of the mouse, larger than she had guessed, standing upright in the grass as if it had expected her, its black eyes meeting her own and the white stripe across its head gleaming in the early sun, stayed her. Some memory, some old human thought teased at her. Instead of striking the mouse, she landed gracefully by its side, her great claws gripping the earth, remembering ground, surrendering to it.

Aki-la. She thought the word again, opened her mouth, and spoke it to the quiet air. She could feel the change begin again. Marrow and sinew and muscle and bone responded, reversing themselves, growing and shrinking, molding and forming. It hurt yet it did not hurt; the pain was delicious.

And still the mouse sat, its bright little eyes watching her until the transformation was complete. Then it squeaked a word, shook itself all over, as if trying to slough off its own skin and bones, and grew, filling earth and sky, resolving itself into a familiar figure with the fierce stare of an eagle and the soft voice of the mouse.

"Late Blossoming Flower," her mother said, and opened welcoming arms to her.

"I have found my word," Flower said as she ran into them. Then, unaccountably, she put her head on her mother's breast and began to sob.

"You have found much more," said her mother. "For see—I have tested you, tempted you to let your animal nature overcome your human nature. And see—you stopped before the hunger for meat, the thirst for blood mastered you and left you forever in your eagle form."

"But I might have killed you," Flower gasped. "I might have eaten you. I was an eagle and you were my natural prey."

"But you did not," her mother said firmly. "Now I must go home."

"Wait," Flower said. "There is something . . . something I have to tell you."

Her mother turned and looked at Flower over her shoulder. "About the old man?"

Flower looked down.

"I know it already. There he is." She pointed to a gray-green butterfly hovering over a blossom. "He is the same undisciplined creature he always was."

"I must change him back. I must learn how, quickly, before he leaves."

"He will not leave," said her mother. "Not that one. Or he would have left our village long ago. No, he will wait until you learn your other powers and change him back so that he may sit on the edge of power and laugh at it as he has always done, as he did to me so long ago. And now, my little one who is my little one no longer, use your eagle wings to fly. I will be waiting at our home for your return."

Flower nodded and then she moved away from her mother and held out her arms. She stretched them as far apart as she could. Even so—even further—would her wings stretch. She looked up into the sky, now blue and cloudless and beckoning.

"*Aki-la!*" she cried, but her mouth was not as stern as her mother's or as that of any of the other women of power, for she still knew how to laugh. She opened her laughing mouth again. "*Aki-la.*"

She felt the change come on her, more easily this time, and she threw herself into the air. The morning sun caught the wash of gold at her neck, like a necklace of power. "*Kya*" she screamed into the waiting wind, "*kya,*" and, for the moment, forgot mother and butterfly and all the land below.

THE SINGER OF SEEDS

Τhere was once a minstrel named Floren who had never held a piece of earth in his hand. He could sing birds out of the trees and milk from a maiden's breast, but of the strong brown soil he knew nothing.

One day, when he came into a small fertile valley named Plaisant and heard the surrounding mountains sing his name, he was more than a little surprised. Still, being a man who believed in signs, he sold his harp for a plow and a plot of land—a poor plow and a strip of earth running close by the mountain foot— and sowed the field.

No one thought he had a hope of a crop, but his strip of land soon began to sprout. He walked up and down the rows singing to his grain, and this was his song:

> *Sunlight and moonbright*
> *And wind through the weeds.*
> *Come up and come over,*

· *The Singer of Seeds* ·

Come up and come over,
Come up and come over
My swift-growing seeds.

At first the neighboring farmers had laughed at Floren and his strange songs. They knew him to be a minstrel, and a good one. He had entertained at their fairs. But he was not a man of the land. His father's father's father had not put in long sweaty years at the plow. So they mocked him, even to his face, and called him Singer of Seeds.

Floren had returned their mockery with a smile, for even he was amused at the dirt under his nails and the way the grain seemed to spring up under his feet. He expected—as they all did— that the few rows would give him no real harvest and that by winter's edge he would be singing in their houses for food. Still, the mountain had called to him and it would have been impolite not to have answered. So he walked the rows of small tender shoots, and sang:

> *"Sunlight and moonbright*
> *And wind through the weeds.*
> *Come up and come over,*
> *Come up and come over,*
> *Come up and come over*
> *My swift-growing seeds."*

After a while he found he loved the sound of his song in the open air, the way it fell against the mountainside and returned to him, the way it seemed to rain down on the new young leaves.

41

After a while, he was content and the soil under his nails seemed natural and good.

But the farmers grew envious of Floren. For though he was no farmer, his plants were growing higher, his corn hardier, his grain fuller than theirs. Though his father's father's fathers had all been wandering minstrels, he was proving to be a better man of the soil than those who had lived all their lives with the soil of Plaisant under their feet. They began to mutter among themselves.

"He does not sing a mere song," one farmer said. "He sings hymns to the devil."

"He does not sing mere hymns to the devil," said another. "He sings an incantation for his crops."

"He does not sing a mere incantation for his own crops," said a third. "He calls out curses on our crops as well."

And so it grew, this seed of envy that the neighboring farmers planted. And by the following spring it was in full flower in their hearts. All they could think of was Floren's luck, for as he flourished so they seemed to decline. And when their early plantings died, flooded out by unusual rains, while Floren's field high on the mountain foot was saved, they knew where to lay the blame.

"It is *his* fault," they said, staring at the drowned crops, as if by not saying his name aloud they would not be accountable for anything that happened.

So they blamed Floren, but they could not decide what they should do.

"Perhaps we should raze his fields," said one.

"We should set his crops ablaze," said another.

"We should send our cattle to trample on his grain."

But though each of them desired revenge, they could not agree on the means. So in the end they agreed to visit the witch who lived in a cave high up in the mountains. She was an old woman who gave nothing but evil advice, and such was their mood, they wanted to hear only the worst.

It was a long climb to her home. For each man the climb seemed endless. Their backs were furrowed with sweat long before they reached the top. And though it was hard enough to climb up alone, each man feared to be left behind so he held onto the shirt of the man in front and, in this way, doubled his agony.

The old witch woman was nearly blind, but the men made enough noise with their curses and cries to tell her they were coming. And so often did they now mix Floren's name in their loud talk, she also knew why they had come. She greeted them when they rounded the last curve, saying, "So you wish to know what to do with that cursed Singer of Seeds."

The men were hot and tired and so their marvel grew. Surely this was a mighty witch, nearly blind yet seeing with such a clear inner eye she had known they were coming and seen their purpose. They did not understand that their own lips and hearts had already betrayed them.

"We wish . . ." they began and then, to a man, stopped.

The old witch smiled at them, waiting. Fear and envy were common enough coins to her. She could afford to wait.

Then one man, braver than the rest, said, "We would end his song."

"Then thrust him from you," advised the witch.

Muttering amongst themselves, the farmers could come to no agreement. At last the same man spoke up again. "He would only return. He claims the mountain sings his name. He says he has sworn to the mountain that he will be with us forever."

They agreed at last. Though none had heard him say it, all believed it had been said. "He swore he would be with us forever," they concurred.

"Then thrust him where he cannot return," said the old woman, making a downward motion with her hand. "Seal his lips with his own mountain and then see if he can sing." She turned her back on the farmers and went into her cave. None of them dared follow.

So there was nothing the tired men could do but go back down the mountain. They grumbled all the way.

Now all the while the farmers had made their way up and then down the mountain, Floren had been at work. He had plowed and furrowed his fields. He had sown his seed. He had weeded and watered and waited for sprouts. And all the while he sang:

> "*Sunlight and moonbright*
> *And wind through the weeds,*
> *Come up and come over,*
> *Come up and come over,*
> *Come up and come over*
> *My swift-growing seeds.*"

Floren's song rose over the fields, over the meadows, up and over the mountain standing jagged against the sky.

The angry farmers, angered even further by their difficult trip down the mountainside, reached their homes late at night. And though they thought it was the ending of that same long day, it had been a season. Such is the way with magic; such is the way with madness.

In the morning when the sun rose, the men rose, too. Each by his own hearth dressed in surly silence. They met by the crossroads that led to Floren's farm.

No one spoke to any other except in growls and signs, for they had almost lost their human tongues. And if by chance a traveler had met them on the path then, he would have thought them a pack of feral men, so fierce were their faces, so wild their eyes.

They came to Floren's farm but he was up before them. It was the time of harvest and he was out with his crops at the sun's first rays. The men were amazed—was it harvest time already? Yet they had left right after planting. They thought the hasty season was magic of Floren's making, though in fact it was they who had climbed throughout the whole growing season, and what they had grown now lay rotted in their hearts.

The farmers lifted their faces to the late summer sun, shrouded in clouds. They sniffed the air. The sounds of Floren's song drifted to them.

"Come up and come over," he sang. "Come up and come over."

The music hurt their ears. One after another they cried out their distress, and the sound was a howling in the wind.

Then they ran into Floren's field, surprising him by his corn, which was full and golden and ripe. Surrounding him, they snapped at him with their teeth and tore at him with their nails. They watched as his life's blood poured out upon the rich dark soil.

Then suddenly the beast in them departed and the sun came out from behind the clouds. Horrified at what they had done, they buried Floren under the field, under the glowing corn. They sealed his lips with the dirt of his own mountain and left, no man daring to look at his neighbor.

The next morning when the sun rose it was pale and thin like a worn copper penny. Every farmer in Plaisant rose, too, hurrying to his own field. But the growing time was over and what little had sprung up in their fields was weedy and scant. Only Floren's field, at the mountain's foot, was full of ripened corn.

As each man looked across his fields, a wind came sighing down the mountainside. It blew a song across Floren's corn field as if on a giant reed pipe. The song was wordless, but each farmer in his field recognized it at once. Floren's corn sang in a thousand voices, as clear as doom:

> *"Sunlight and moonbright*
> *And wind through the weeds.*
> *Come up and come over,*
> *Come up and come over,*
> *Come up and come over*
> *My swift-growing seeds."*

It sang on and on that year and every year for the rest of their lives.

Every season from that time on, the corn grew without planting in Floren's field, and every season it sang his song. The wind whistled his song across the valley of Plaisant. And though passers-by thought it a pleasant, cheerful song, the farmers heard a different tune. Floren was indeed with them forever.

ATLAS

*B*ut I have shrugged and tried to shift
My burden to another's back,
To one more used to bear.

Yet still it presses on my neck.
The highest mountains wear
Crevices in my shoulders and sweat

Mingles with the rivers. I let
Unbidden waters drip through my hair
And meander in sharp turns

Across my forehead. As I lift
This world, a god racked
In immortal torture,

I wish for some swift death,
Or that this heavy world would crack
For I am man enough to care.

THE BOY WHO DREW
UNICORNS

There was once a boy who drew unicorns. Even before he knew their names, he caught them mane and hoof and horn on his paper. And they were white beasts and gray, black beasts and brown, galloping across the brown supermarket bags. He didn't know what to call them at first, but he knew what they called him: Phillip, a lover of horses, Philly, Phil.

Now children, there is going to be a new boy in class today. His name is Philadelphia Carew.

Philadelphia? That's a city name not a kid's name.

Hey, my name is New York.

Call me Chicago.

I got a cousin named India, does that count?

Enough, children. This young man is very special. You must try to be kind to him. He'll be very shy. And he's had a lot of family problems.

I got family problems too, Ms. Wynne. I got a brother and he's a big problem.

48

Joseph, that's enough.

He's six feet tall. That's a very *big problem.*

Now you may all think you have problems, but this young man has more than most. You see, he doesn't talk.

Not ever?

No. But not now. Not for several years. That's close enough to ever, I think.

Bet you'd like it if we didn't talk for several years.

No, I wouldn't like that at all, though if I could shut you up for several hours, Joseph . . .

Oooooh, Joey, she's got you!

"What is the good of such drawing, Philadelphia?" his mother said. "If you have to draw, draw something useful. Draw me some money or some groceries or a new man. One who doesn't beat us. Draw us some better clothes or a bed for yourself. Draw me a job."

But he drew only unicorns: horse-like, goat-like, deer-like, lamb-like, bull-like, things he had seen in books. Four-footed, silken swift, with the single golden horn. His part of the apartment was papered with them.

When's he coming, Ms. Wynne?

Today. After lunch.

Does he look weird, too?

He's not weird, Joseph. He's special. And I expect you—all of you—to act special.

She means we shouldn't talk.

No, Joseph, I mean you need *to think before you talk. Think what it must be like not to be able to express yourself.*

49

I'd use my hands.
Does he use his hands, Ms. Wynne?
I don't know.
Stupid, only deaf people do that. Is he deaf?
No.
Is there something wrong with his tongue?
No.
Why doesn't he talk, then?
Why do you think?
Maybe he likes being special.
That's a very interesting idea, Joseph.
Maybe he's afraid.
Afraid to talk? Don't be dumb.
Now, Joseph, that's another interesting idea, too. What are you afraid of, children?
Snakes, Ms. Wynne.
I hate spiders.
I'm not afraid of anything!
Nothing at all, Joseph?
Maybe my big brother. When he's mad.

In school he drew unicorns down the notebook page, next to all his answers. He drew them on his test papers. On the bathroom walls. They needed no signature. Everyone knew he had made them. They were his thumbprints. They were his heartbeats. They were his scars.

Oooooh, he's drawing them things again.
Don't you mess up my paper, Mr. Philadelphia Carew.

50

Leave him alone. He's just a dummy.
Horses don't have horns, dummy.
Here comes Ms. Wynne.
If you children will get back in your seats and stop crowding
around Philly. You've all seen him draw unicorns before. Now
listen to me, and I mean you too, Joseph. Fold your hands and
lift those shining faces to me. Good. We are going on a field trip
this afternoon. Joseph, sit in your seat properly and leave Philly's
paper alone. A field trip to Chevril Park. Not now, Joseph. Get
back in your seat. We will be going after lunch. And *after your*
spelling test.
Ooooh, what test, Ms. Wynne?
You didn't say there was going to be a test.

The park was a place of green glades. It had trees shaped like
ice cream bars with the chocolate running down the sides. It had
trees like umbrellas that moved mysteriously in the wind. There
were hidden ponds and secret streams and moist pathways between, lined with rings of white toadstools and trillium the color
of blood. Cooing pigeons walked boldly on the pavement. But in
the quiet underbrush hopped little brown birds with white throats.
Silent throats.

From far away came a strange, magical song. It sounded like
a melody mixed with a gargle, a tune touched by a laugh. It
creaked, it hesitated, then it sang again. He had never heard
anything like it before.

I hear it, Ms. Wynne. I hear the merry-go-round.
And what does it sound like, children?

51

It sounds lumpy.
Don't be dumb. It sounds upsy-downsy.
It sounds happy and sad.
Joseph, what do you think it sounds like?
Like another country. Like The Twilight Zone.
Very good, Joseph. And see, Philly is agreeing with you. And
strangely, Joseph, you are right. Merry-go-rounds or carousels
are from another country, another world. The first ones were
built in France in the late 1700s. The best hand-carved animals
still are made in Europe. What kind of animals do you think
you'll see on this merry-go-round?
Horses.
Lions.
Tigers.
Camels.
Don't be dumb—camels.
Are too! I been here before. And *elephants.*

He saw unicorns, galloping around and around, a whole herd
of them. And now he saw his mistake. They were not like horses
or goats or deer or lambs or bulls. They were like—themselves.
And with the sun slanting on them, from beyond the trees, they
were like rainbows, all colors and no colors at all.

Their mouths were open and they were calling. That was the
magical song he had heard before. A strange, shimmery kind of
cry, not like horses or goats or deer or lambs or bulls; more
musical, with a strange rise and fall to each phrase.

He tried to count them as they ran past. Seven, fifteen, twenty-
one . . . he couldn't contain them all. Sometimes they doubled

back and he was forced to count them again. And again. He settled for the fact that it was a herd of unicorns. No. *Herd* was too ordinary a word for what they were. Horses came in herds. And cows. But unicorns—there had to be a special word for them all together. Suddenly he knew what it was, as if they had told him so in their wavery song. He was watching a *surprise* of unicorns.

Look at old weird Philly. He's just staring at the merry-go-round. Come on, Mr. Philadelphia Chicago New York L.A. Carew. Go on up and ride. They won't bite.

Joseph, keep your mouth shut and you might be able to hear something.

What, Ms. Wynne?

You might hear the heart's music, Joseph. That's a lot more interesting than the flapping of one's own mouth.

What does that mean, Ms. Wynne?

It means shut up, Joseph.

Ooooh, she got you, Joey.

It means shut up, Denise, too, I bet.

All of you, mouths shut, ears open. We're going for a ride.

We don't have any money, Ms. Wynne.

That's all taken care of. Everyone pick out a horse or a whatever. Mr. Frangipanni, the owner of this carousel, can't wait all day.

Dibs on the red horse.

I got the gray elephant.

Mine's the white horse.

No, Joseph, can't you see Philly has already chosen that one?

But the superheroes always ride the white horse. And he isn't any kind of superhero.

Choose another one, Joseph.

Aaaah, Ms. Wynne, that's not fair.

Why not take the white elephant, Joseph. Hannibal, a great hero of history, marched across the high Alps on elephants to capture Rome.

Wow—did he really?

Really, Joseph.

Okay. Where's Rome?

Who knows where Rome is? I bet Mr. Frangipanni does.

Then ask Mr. Frangipanni!

Italy, Ms. Wynne.

Italy is right. Time to mount up. That's it. We're all ready, Mr. Frangipanni.

The white flank scarcely trembled, but he saw it. Do not be afraid, he thought. I couldn't ever hurt you. He placed his hand gently on the tremor and it stopped.

Moving up along the length of the velvety beast, he saw the arched neck ahead of him, its blue veins like tiny rivers branching under the angel-hair mane.

One swift leap and he was on its back. The unicorn turned its head to stare at him with its amber eyes. The horn almost touched his knee. He flinched, pulling his knee up close to his chest. The unicorn turned its head back and looked into the distance.

He could feel it move beneath him, the muscles bunching and flattening as it walked. Then with that strange wild cry, the unicorn leaped forward and began to gallop around and around the glade.

He could sense others near him, catching movement out of the corners of his eyes. Leaning down, he clung to the unicorn's mane. They ran through day and into the middle of night till the stars fell like snow behind them. He heard a great singing in his head and heart and he suddenly felt as if the strength of the old kings were running in his blood. He threw his head back and laughed aloud.

Boy, am I dizzy.
My elephant was the best.
I had a red pony. Wow, did we fly!
Everyone dismounted? Now, tell me how you felt.

He slid off the silken side, feeling the solid earth beneath his feet. There was a buzz of voices around him, but he ignored them all. Instead, he turned back to the unicorn and walked toward its head. Standing still, he reached up and brought its horn down until the point rested on his chest. The golden whorls were hard and cold beneath his fingers. And if his fingers seemed to tremble ever so slightly, it was no more than the unicorn's flesh had shuddered once under the fragile shield of its skin.

He stared into the unicorn's eyes, eyes of antique gold so old he wondered if they had first looked on the garden where the original thrush had sung the first notes from a hand-painted bush.

Taking his right hand off the horn, he sketched a unicorn in the air between them.

As if that were all the permission it needed, the unicorn nodded its head. The horn ripped his light shirt, right over the heart. He put his left palm over the rip. The right he held out to the unicorn. It nuzzled his hand and its breath was moist and warm.

Look, look at Philly's shirt.
Ooooh, there's blood.
Let me through, children. Thank you, Joseph, for helping him get down. Are you hurt, Philly? Now don't be afraid. Let me see. I could never hurt you. Why, I think there's a cut there. Mr. Frangipanni, come quick. Have you any bandages? The boy is hurt. It's a tiny wound but there's lots of blood so it may be very deep. Does it hurt, dear?

No.

Brave boy. Now be still till Mr. Frangipanni comes.
He spoke, Ms. Wynne. Philly spoke.
Joseph, do be still, I have enough trouble without you . . .
But he spoke, Ms. Wynne. He said "no."
Don't be silly, Joseph.
But he did. He spoke. Didn't you, Philly?
Yes.

Yes.
He turned and looked.
The unicorn nodded its head once and spoke in that high, wavering magical voice. "THE HORN HEALS."
He repeated it.

Yes. The horn heals.
He spoke! He spoke!
I'll just clean this wound, Philly, don't move. Why—that's strange. There's some blood, but only an old scar. Are you sure you're all right, dear?
Yes.

Yes.

As he watched, the unicorn dipped its horn to him once, then whirled away, disappearing into the dappled light of the trees. He wondered if he would ever capture it right on paper. It was nothing like the sketches he had drawn before. Nothing. But he would try.

Yes, Ms. Wynne, an old scar healed. I'm sure.

SIR JOHN MANDEVILLE'S
REPORT ON THE GRIFFIN

PERSIA, 12TH CENTURY

hiking in the Scythian hills,
John Mandeville stops for his tea,
Unpacks his hamper, eats his scones,
Surveys the land for a rarity,
Some miracle, some un-nature
To make this trip to Araby
  The cause for royalty's delight,
  So that he might become a knight.

The air is heavy, hot, and still,
Yet Mandeville hears overhead
The shuttering of metallic wings.
(In ether are the best dreams bred.)
The hamper holds more than his tea.
He scatters on the ground the bread
  That he has brought, the bloody meat
  Which predators will find a treat.

58

· *Sir John Mandeville's Report on the Griffin* ·

Then he sits down, his pen in hand
To wait upon the mythic beast
And capture it upon the page
While it chokes down his proffered feast.
The ink dries up long, long before
Our John's imaginings have ceased.
   The foolscap tells an eerie tale
   Of griffin wing and tooth and nail.

"They have the shape," he scribbles down,
"Eagle before, lion behind."
His eager pen invents the form,
Remarks the species, clan, and kind;
Recounts the fierceness of the race
That guards the gold the gods have mined.
   His travelogue has just the wit
   To make the facts all sort-of fit.

And when the clattering wings depart,
And once again the land is clean,
He finishes his travel notes
And makes quite certain that they mean
A metaphor to please the king,
A parable to tempt the queen.
   Ignoring what his eyes behold,
   A different tale is what he's told.

The transformation on the page,
The careful building blocks of diction,

Cause our traveler little pain
Nor cause his heart the slightest friction.
He knows well the audience
For his attempts at science fiction.
   His work at home will not be slighted.
   And for his travel book he's knighted.

MORAL:

   The moral of this tale is given:
   Where you see eagle, there write griffin.

WOLF/CHILD

The sun was a red eye staring over the farthest hills when the she-wolf came back from the hunt. She ran easily into the jungle undergrowth on a path only she knew. As she entered the canopied sal forest, the tight lacings of leaves shut out the light. Shadows of shadows played along the tall branchless trunks of the trees.

The guinea fowl she carried in her mouth was still warm, though she had been almost an hour running with it. She had neither savaged nor eaten a portion. It was all for her cubs, the three who were ready to hunt on their own and the two light-colored hairless ones who still suckled though they had been with her through two litters before this one. There would be good eating tonight.

The she-wolf stopped twenty feet from her den, crouching low under a plum bush and measuring the warm with her nose. The musky odor of tiger still lingered shoulder-high on the *pipal* trunk, but it was an old casting. And there was no other danger riding the wind.

She looked around once, trusting her eyes only at the very last, and then she ran, crouched belly down, over to the beveled remains of the white ant mound. Slipping past another plum bush that all but obscured the entrance, she crawled down the twisting main passage, ignoring the smaller veins, to the central den. There, on the earth floor she had scratched and smoothed herself, were the waiting cubs.

The three weanlings greeted her arrival with open-mouthed smiles and stayed on their bellies, waiting for their shares of the meal. But the smaller of the hairless cubs crawled over and reached out for the bird with one pink paw.

The she-wolf dropped the bird and put her own paw on it, gently biting the hairless one on the top of the nose. At that, the cub seemed to shrink back into itself. It whined and, mouth open, rolled over on its back. Its bare pink belly, streaked with dirt, moved rapidly up and down with each breath. It whimpered.

The she-wolf gave a sharp bark of assent and the hairless cub rolled over on its stomach and sat up.

At the bark, the four other cubs came to her side. They watched, eyes shining with night-sight, as she gobbled down sections of the bird and chewed each piece thoroughly. Then she regurgitated back the soft pieces for each of them. The larger hairless cub gathered up several of the biggest sections and brought one over to its small twin.

Soon the only sound in the den far underground was that of chewing. The she-wolf gnawed on the small bones.

When the meal was finished, the she-wolf turned around three times before settling. When she lay down the three hairy cubs came to nuzzle at her side, but she pushed them away. They were ready to be weaned and it would not do for them to suck more. She had but a trickle of milk left and knew the cubs needed that slight edge of hunger to help them learn to hunt.

But the other cubs were different. Their sucking had never been as hard or as painful when the milk teeth had given way to the sharper incisors. They had never hurt her or fought their brothers for a place at the teat. Rather they waited until the others slept, moving them off the still-swollen milkbag with gentle pushes. Somehow, through three litters they had never nursed enough.

The she-wolf made room for the two hairless cubs to lie down by her side. The smaller cub nursed, patting the she-wolf with grimed paws. It gave soft bubbly sighs, a sound that had once seemed alien to the she-wolf but was now as familiar as the grunting sounds of the other cubs. She licked diffidently at the strange matting on the cub's head, all tangled and full of burrs. Each time she took the cubs outside, the matting was harder to clean. The she-wolf seemed to remember a time when the two had been completely without hair. But memory was not her way. She stopped licking after a while, lay back, closed her eyes, and slept.

When the little cub finished nursing, the older one moved cautiously next to it, curled around it, and then fell asleep to dream formlessly in a succession of broken images.

"There is a *manush-bagha*, sahib," the small brown man said to the soldier sitting behind the desk. The native held his palms together while he spoke, less an attitude of prayer than one of fear. With his hands apart, the soldier would see how they trembled.

"What does he mean?" Turning to his subaltern, the man behind the desk shook his head. "I can't understand these native dialects."

"A man-ghost, sir. It's a belief some of the more primitive forest tribes hold." The younger man smiled, hoping for approval from both the colonel and the native. "A *manush-bagha* can be the ghost of some dead native or . . ."

"By God, a revenant!" the colonel exclaimed. "I've always wanted to find one. My aunt was supposed to have one in her dressing room—the ghost of a maid who hanged herself. But she never manifested while I was there."

". . . or, in some cases," the young soldier continued, "it can be dangerous." He paused. "Or so the natives believe."

"Better and better," murmured the colonel.

"They are eaters of flesh," the brown man said suddenly, hands still together, and eyes now wide.

"Eaters of *flesh*?" asked the colonel.

The native lowered his eyes quickly and said very quietly, "The *manush-bagha* eats human beings." After a beat, he added, "Sahib."

"Splendid!" said the colonel. "That caps it. We'll go." He turned to his subaltern. "Geoffrey, lay it on for tomorrow morning. I want beaters, the proper number of guns, and maps. And get this one," he pointed to the brown-skinned man before him, "to give you precise directions. *Precise.*" He stood. "Not that they know the meaning of the word." With a quick step he left the room, oblivious to his subaltern's snapped salute or the bow of the native or the long glance that followed between them.

The she-wolf listened to the soft breathing of her cubs and quietly moved away from them. She padded past the sleeping forms and wound her way through the tunnels of the white ant mound and out the second entrance to her den. In the darkening forest her gray-brown coat blended into the shadows.

Above in the sal canopy a colony of langurs, tails curled like question marks over their backs, scolded one another, loudly warning of her intrusion. She turned her head to look at them and they moved off together, leaping from branch to branch to branch. The branches swayed with their passage, but the trunks of the trees, mottled with gray and green lichens, never moved.

A covey of partridge flew up before her, a noisy exaltation. Two great butterflies floated by, just out of reach, their velvety black wings pumping gracefully, making no noise.

The she-wolf paused for a moment to watch the silent passage of the butterflies, then she turned to the east and was gone quickly into the underbrush.

When she returned to the den over an hour later, she had another plump guinea hen in her mouth, one feather comically stuck to her nose. Tonight there would be good eating.

The colonel and his subaltern rode in the bullock cart, moving slowly through the forest. Hours before they had left the neat, green rice swamps to cross the countryside toward the sal.

"A barren waste," the colonel said, dismissing the grayish land.

Geoffrey refrained from pointing to the herons that stalked along the single strand rivers or reminding the colonel of the low croaking of the hundreds of frogs. Not barren, he thought to himself, but with a different kind of richness. He said nothing.

The native guiding them told Geoffrey his name was Raman, though he had told the colonel, he was called Ramanrithan. He walked ahead of the bullock cart to help lead the cranky beasts, while the two hired carters went on ahead of them with axes. In this particular part of the sal forest vines grew up quickly across old pathways. Every day fresh routes had to be cut.

The swaying of the cart had a soporific effect on the colonel, who nodded off, but Geoffrey refused to sleep. Being new to the sal, though he had read several books about it, he wanted to take it all in.

The canopy was so thick, it was hard to tell whether or not the sun was overhead, and the only light was a kind of filtered green. A magical sense of unpassed time possessed the young subaltern, and he drew in a deep breath. The sound of it joined the *racheta-racheta* of the stick that protruded from the empty kerosene can the carters had affixed under the wagon. As the stick struck the cart wheels it produced a steady noise which, the carters assured them, would frighten away any of the larger predators.

"Tigers do not like it, Sahib," the carter had said. Geoffrey hadn't liked it either. It seemed to violate the jungle's sanctity. But after a while, he stopped hearing it as a separate noise. At one point the path was so overgrown, the carters and Raman could barely cut their way through, and Geoffrey joined them, first stripping down to his vest. As his arm swung up and back with its axe, he noticed for the first time how white his own skin seemed next to theirs, though he had acquired a deep tan by Cambridge standards. But his arms looked somehow unnatural to him in the jungle setting.

At last they completed their task and stopped, all at once, to congratulate one another. At that very moment, Geoffrey heard the low cough of a tiger. He started back toward the cart where his gun rested against the wheel.

One of the carters called out to him. "It is very far away, Sahib, and you must not worry."

Geoffrey smiled his thanks and walked away from the three men in order to go down the path a little ways by himself. When he looked up, there was a peacock above him, on a swing of vine. He could remember nothing in England that had so moved him. He stood for a moment watching it, then abruptly turned back. When he got to the cart the colonel was awake.

"For God's sake, man, put on your shirt. It won't do."

Geoffrey put on his shirt and climbed back up in the cart. The noise of the stick against the wheels began again, drowning out everything else.

The colonel was refreshed by his nap and showed it by his running commentary. "These natives," he said with a nod that took in both the carters, who were city-bred, and Raman, "are all so superstitious, Geoffrey. And timid. They have to be led by us or they'd get nothing done. But, by God, if there *is* some kind of ghost I want to see it. That's not superstition. There are many odd things out here in the jungle. I could write it up. Major General Sleeman did that, you know. Field notes. About the oddities seen. It just takes an observant eye, my boy. I took a first at Oxford. What do you think, Geoffrey?"

But before Geoffrey could answer, the colonel continued, "*Manushies.* Man-eaters. Silly buggers. Probably only some kind of ape. But if it were some *new* sort of ape, that would be one for the books, now wouldn't it? A carnivorous ape. Probably that, rather than a ghost, though . . ." and his voice turned wistful, "I never did see my Aunt Evelyn's ghost. A maid, she was, got caught out by one of the sub-gardeners. Hanged herself in the pantry. Aunt Evelyn swears by her."

Geoffrey had fallen asleep.

*   *   *

The she-wolf stood by the entrance to the white ant mound and called softly. The cubs came out one by one. Overhead a slight breeze stirred the canopy of leaves, and green fruit pigeons called across the dusky clearing, a soft, low sound.

The first cubs out were the three weanlings, sliding belly down out through the entrance hole, and then stretching. The two hairless cubs crept out after, their light brown muzzle-faces peering around alertly. The she-wolf stalked over to her cubs and as if at a signal, they knelt before her, wagging their tails.

She gave a sharp high yip and they stood, following her out of the clearing. They went past the great mohua tree and into the tangled underbrush which closed behind them so quickly there was no sign that any creature had passed that way.

Raman held a sal leaf in his palm as they walked along. He said he could tell how much time had passed by the withering of the leaf. Geoffrey timed it with his pocket watch and was amazed at how accurate the little man's calculations were.

"And how long now until we get to your village?" Geoffrey asked.

Raman looked up at a stray ray of sun that had found itself through a tear in the canopy, then looked down at the leaf in his hand. "Before dark," he said.

Geoffrey repeated this to the colonel and told him about the withering leaf.

"Silly buggers," said the colonel. "What will they think of next to twit you, Geoffrey? Of course the man knows how long it takes to get to his village. The leaf is sheer flummery."

*   *   *

The she-wolf led the cubs to the edge of a clearing where a herd of reddish-brown chital grazed. One of the cubs, excited by the deer, yipped. At the sound, the herd ran off leaving a thick smoky cloud of dust behind. The pack circled the clearing, five small shadows behind the she-wolf. At the southern end of the open area, she dropped suddenly to her stomach and the cubs did likewise.

As they watched, a strange noisy man-cart crossed the clearing, accompanied by a dreadful sound. *Racheta-racheta-racheta*. The pack did not move until long after the cart had passed. The she-wolf growled and her cubs crept beneath a pipal tree and waited, lying heads down on their front paws. Only when she was sure they would not leave the shelter of the tree did she check out the trail the bullock cart had left behind. There were deep ruts in the grass and the underbrush was broken. The smell of the cart was sharp, but there was something slightly familiar about it, too.

The she-wolf sniffed one more time, then loped back to her cubs. At her bark they rose and followed. She was careful to avoid the broken grasses and the cart smell, which offended her nose. The deep meat smell bespoke of an animal too large for a single wolf to handle. She knew they would have to range further.

But after coursing the jungle with the cubs for most of the night, the she-wolf had still made no kill. There would be no good eating this night. She shepherded them back to the white ant mound where, after nuzzling them all, she allowed them to suck until they were full.

The men of Raman's village ran out to greet the cart through green clumps of bamboo that hid the adobe-and-thatch houses. Much to Geoffrey's embarrassment, the men insisted on washing the visitors' feet, but the colonel took it with a certain graciousness.

"Let them do it, Geoffrey," he said placidly. "It does no harm, and it certainly keeps them in their place. But stop blushing, boy. Your face is too wide open. It's like a damned girl's."

After the washing, they replaced their socks and boots, and threaded their way down the packed dirt street, the colonel greeting everyone with a kind of official *bonhomie* that Geoffrey found himself envying. Raman strode ahead to announce them. With the noise of the cart and the bellowing of the bewildered bullock and the nasal whine of *narh* pipes, it was a wild processional.

Near the end of the village was a rather larger hut, and this, Raman assured them, was where the most welcome visitors would stay. The carters would be put up elsewhere. Two women in white saris with brass pitchers on their hips nodded as Geoffrey got down from the cart. The colonel was last to dismount and as his feet touched the ground, there was a low admiring murmur. He smiled.

"Ask them, Geoffrey, what time dinner is served."

Dinner was served immediately, and though the English retired early, the villagers stayed up well into the night entertaining the carters with rice beer and Raman's boasts about how the colonel would kill the *manush-baghas* the next day.

When they woke in the morning, quite early according to Geoffrey's watch, the village day had already begun.

The mohua tree loomed over the clearing like an ancient giant, its trunk crisscrossed with claw marks. All day the noise of hammers and the shouts of men dominated the clearing, but the she-wolf and her cubs did not hear them. They were deep in the den, sealed off by sleep and the twisting tunnels of the white ant mound. By dusk when they were ready to go out into the woods to hunt, the men were long departed. Only the *machan*, some twenty feet up the mohua tree, gave mute evidence that they had been there. That and the scattered pieces of wood and broken branches.

The she-wolf, in the darkness of her den, stretched and stood. Two of the cubs were awake before her and they danced around her legs until she cuffed one of them still. Roughly she licked awake the other three. The smallest of the hairless cubs whimpered for a moment, but at last she, too, stood.

They scampered around the winding tunnel until they came to the entrance. Then they waited until the she-wolf went out first into the darkening world.

Three miles from the village was the clearing where the *manush-baghas* had been sighted.

"Always at dusk, sahib," explained Raman. "Only at dusk."

That was why the villagers had gone on ahead early in the day to build a *machan*, a shooting platform, in the only large tree in the clearing, an ancient mohua. They had finished the makeshift *machan* by noon, and had hurried home, feeling terribly brave and proud.

Picking up his smoothbore, the colonel turned to Geoffrey. "Well, it's up to us now."

Geoffrey nodded. "Raman will take us to the clearing," he said, "but he will not stay the night. He is too afraid."

"Well, tell him we are not afraid. We are English," Geoffrey told him.

"And tell him he should come in the morning with several others and we shall have his *manushie* for him." The colonel smiled.

"Do you have that cage out of the cart? We shall have to carry it there. Don't want the noise of that blasted cart to scare away the ape. Raman shall have to carry it."

Geoffrey nodded and turned to give the instructions to Raman and the others who had gathered to see them off. Then, in a modest processional, quite unlike the one of the evening before, they went down the packed dirt road and off to the west.

There was much more of a path at first, and even when the path gave way to hacked jungle, so many men had been there just hours before that the walking was easy. Raman, who shouldered the cage without complaint, slipped easily along the walkway, and they followed, reaching the clearing well before dusk.

Some thirty yards from the mohua tree, near a stand of black-thorn, was a termite mound that looked very much like an Indian temple. Next to it were the remains of another mound that had been destroyed by the last rainy season.

"There, sahib, that is where the man-ghost lives," whispered Raman, letting the cage off his back and wrestling it to the foot of the mohua tree. "At night it will come. The *manush-bagha*."

"Very good, Raman. You may go now," said the colonel. He chuckled as Raman took him literally and fled the clearing. "Well, well," the colonel added. He walked over to the termite mound and walked around it slowly and thoughtfully.

"Would an ape live in there?" asked Geoffrey uncomfortably.

"Would a ghost?"

They circled the mound again, this time in silence. Then the colonel nodded his head back toward the mohua tree. When they were beneath it, the colonel looked up. "Time to settle ourselves."

Leaving the lantern at the foot of the tree, the colonel climbed up the rope ladder first and Geoffrey followed.

"I think," the colonel said, when they were settled on the wooden platform, "that the drill now is no more talking. Load your gun, my boy, and then we will sit watch."

They finished their few preparations and then sat silently, eyes trained on the white ant mound. Geoffrey had to fight off the impulse to swing his legs over the side of the *machan*, which reminded him of a tree fort he and his brothers had built in an ancient oak beside his Malvern home.

The darkness moved in quietly, casting long shadows. The hum of the cicadas was mesmerizing, and they both had to shake their heads frequently to stay awake.

And then, suddenly, something moved by the mound, near a plum bush. Head up, sniffing the air, a full-grown wolf emerged.

Geoffrey felt a hand on his arm, but he did not look around. Slowly he raised his gun as the colonel raised his, and they waited.

Three cubs scampered around the bush. One dashed toward the blackthorn and a sharp yip from the she-wolf recalled him. The cubs scuffled at their mother's feet.

And then, as if on signal, they all stopped playing and looked at the plum bush.

Geoffrey drew in a deep breath that was noisy only to his own ears. The colonel did not move at all.

From behind the bush a small childlike form came forth. It had an enormous bushy head and its honey arms and legs were knobbed and scarred.

"The ape!" whispered the colonel as he fired.

His first shot hit the she-wolf on the shoulder, spinning her around. At the noise, wood pigeons rose up from the trees, their wings making a clacketing sound. The colonel's second shot blew away half the wolf's head, from the ear to the muzzle. He leaped up, shaking the *machan*, crowing, "Got her!"

The three cubs disappeared back behind the bush, but the *manush-bagha* went over to the wolf's body and pawed at it mournfully. Then it dipped its face into the blood and, raising the bloody mask toward the mohua tree, found Geoffrey's eyes. Unaccountably he wanted to weep. Then the creature put its head back and howled.

"Shoot it!" the colonel said. "Geoffrey, shoot it!"

Geoffrey lowered his gun and shook his head. "It's a child, colonel," he whispered as the creature scuttled off behind the plum bush. "A child."

"Ah, you bloody fool," the colonel said in disgust. "Now we shall have to track it." Gun in hand, he clambered awkwardly down the rope ladder and strode over to the bush. Geoffrey followed uneasily.

Poking his gun into the bush, the colonel let out a short, barking laugh. "There's a hole here, Geoffrey. Come see. An entrance of some kind. Ha-ha! They've gone to ground."

Geoffrey shuddered, though he did not know why. The clearing suddenly seemed filled with an alien presence, a darkness he could not quite name. He knew night came quickly in the jungle once the sun began its descent, but it was more than that. The clearing was very still.

The colonel had begun ripping away the branches that obscured the hole, his gun laid by. "Come on, Geoffrey, give us a hand."

Geoffrey put his own gun down, and found himself whispering

a prayer he had learned so many years ago in the little stone church near his home, a prayer against "the waiters in the dark." Then he bent to help the colonel clear away the bush.

The hole did not go plumb down but was a tunnel on the slant, heading back toward the termite mound. After a moment of digging with his hands, the colonel straightened up.

"There!" he said pointing to the mound. "It's a bolt hole from that thing. I'll guard this hole, Geoffrey, and you go and start digging out that mound."

Reluctantly, Geoffrey did as he was told. The termite mound stood higher than his head and when he tried to scrape away the dirt, he found it was hardened from the days and months in the rain. He cast around and found a large branch that had fallen from one of the blackthorn trees. With a mighty swing, he sent the branch crashing into the mound, decapitating the mound and shattering the stick.

Scrambling up the side, he peered down into the mound but it was still too dark to see much, so he pulled away great handsful of dirt from the inside out. After frantic minutes of digging, he had managed to carve the mound down until it was a waist-high pit.

The colonel came over to help. "I've blocked off that bolt hole," he said. "They won't be getting out *that* way. What do you have?" His face was slick with sweat and there were two dark spots on his cheeks, as if he burned with fever.

Geoffrey was too winded to talk, and pointed to the pit. But just then complete darkness closed in, so the colonel made his way back to the foot of the mohua where he found the lantern. It flared into light and sent trembling shadows leaping about the mound. When he held it directly over the open pit, they could make out five forms—the three cubs and not one but two of the apelike creatures wrapped together into a great monkey ball. At the light, they all buried their heads except for the largest. That one looked up, glaring into the light, its eyes sparkling a kind of red fire. Lifting its lips back from large yellow teeth, it growled.

The colonel laughed. "I'll stay here and guard this bunch. They won't be going anywhere. You run back to the village and get our carters. And that Ramanrithan fellow."

"They won't come here after dark," Geoffrey protested. "And which of us shall have the lantern?"

"Don't talk nonsense," the colonel said. "You take the lantern and tell them I've captured not one but two of their *manushies* and I'm not afraid to stay here in the dark with them. Tell those silly villagers they have nothing to fear. The British *Sahib* is on the job." He laughed out loud again.

"Are you sure . . . ?" Geoffrey began.

"One of England's finest scared silly of three wolf cubs and a pair of feral children?" the colonel asked.

"Then you knew . . . ?" Geoffrey began, wondering just when it was the colonel had realized they were not apes, and not wanting to ask.

"All along, Geoffrey," the colonel said. "All along." He patted the subaltern on the shoulder, a fatherly gesture that would have been out of place had they not been alone and in the dark clearing. "Now don't you get the willies, my boy, like those silly brown men. Color is the difference, Geoffrey. They've no stamina, no guts, and lots of bloody superstitions. Run along, and fetch them back."

Geoffrey picked up the lantern, shouldered his smoothbore, and started back down the path.

*   *   *

The cubs shivered together, trying to remember the feel of their mother's warmth, knowing something was missing. The little hairless cub cried out in hunger. But the larger one closed her eyes, playing back the moment when the she-wolf's head had burst apart like a piece of fruit thrown down by the langurs. She recalled the taste of the blood, both sweet and salt in her mouth. Turning her head slightly, she sniffed the air. Mother was gone but Mother was here. There would be good eating tonight.

By the time Geoffrey could convince the villagers that the colonel had everything under control, it was already dawn and they were willing to come anyway. But they brought rakes and sticks for protection and made Geoffrey march on ahead.

The path had grown almost completely shut in the few hours since he had passed that way. He marveled at the jungle's constancy. Around him, the green walls hid an incredible prolix life, only now and again pulling aside a viny curtain to showcase one creature or another.

The tight lacings of the sal above showed little light, only occasional streaks of sun. From far away he could hear the scolding of langurs moving through the treetops. Behind him the villagers muttered and giggled, and it seemed much hotter than the day before.

When they got near the clearing, Geoffrey called out into the quiet, but the colonel did not answer. The men behind him began to talk among themselves uneasily. Geoffrey signaled them to be still, and moved on ahead.

By the termite mound lay a body.

Geoffrey ran over to it. The colonel lay as if he had been thrown down from a great height, yet there was nothing he might have been thrown down from. Horribly, his face and hands had been savaged, mutilated. "Eaten away," Geoffrey whispered to himself. Even the nose bone had been cracked. Yet remarkably, his clothing was little disturbed.

Turning aside, Geoffrey was quietly and efficiently sick, not caring if the villagers saw him. Then, wiping his mouth on his sleeve, he peered over into the mound. The cubs and the children were as he had left them, in that tight monkey ball, asleep. Thank God they had not been molested by whatever beast or beasts had savaged the colonel.

Bending over the mound, and crooning so as not to frighten them, Geoffrey pried away the littlest child and picked her up. The stink of her was ghastly, an unwashed carrion smell. She trembled in his arms. Patting her matted hair gingerly, he cuddled her in his arms and at last she stopped shivering and began to nuzzle at his neck, making a low almost purring sound. She weighed no more than one of his nieces, who were two and three years old.

"Here," Geoffrey called out to the villagers, his back to the colonel's mutilated corpse, "come see. It is only a child gone wild in the jungle. And there is another one here as well. We must take them home. Cleaned up they'll be just like other children." But when he looked over, he realized he spoke to an empty clearing as, from behind him, there came a strange and terrible growl.

She comforted the cubs who still trembled in the light, patting them and licking their fur. Deep in her throat she made the mother sound. "*Very* good eating today."

THE MAKING OF DRAGONS

If only it were still simple,
fire, water, earth, air,
                    the staples
of the older gods. But modern days
require choice, that modern phrase.
So choose—good dragon, bad dragon, west or east.
We must prioritize your beast.
You buy your myth with hollow coins.
So choose:
            fire in the mouth or in the loins.

THE HEAD:
            the placement of the jagged teeth,
the poison glands, above, beneath
the forking tongue.
                    Eyes that spark fire?
The mouth, when open, breathing desire?
The jaw reticulated, viz. the snake.

79

The voice articulated, viz. the crake.
The tone: a cry, a scream, a roar?
In the making of dragons less is not more.

THE TRUNK:
> *the body comes in three basic styles.*
One, the sinuous body that goes on for miles
(or metres in our continental design).
That is our Ororoborus line.
Two, the stumpy, humpy dinosaur
which will cost you a bit more
but comes with guarantees in parts replacement.
(We keep a year's supply in our basement.)
The third, imported from the east,
well, we recommend that one the least.

THE TAIL:
> *caudal vertebrae aside,*
a tail can be narrow or it can be wide,
it can be flexible or it can be hard,
used for a rudder, a weapon, a guard,
but all tails must be a certain length
to guarantee balance, poise, and strength.
Here is the formula (or as we say in the trade, the key):

Length from nose to sacrum $+ 2 \times 2\frac{1}{2}$ equals tail

or

$$NSL + 2 \times 2.5 = T$$

· *The Making of Dragons* ·

OPTIONS:
        scales, feathers, skin, or fur.
Sexes: him, it, hermaphro, her.
Nails: oak, teak, ivory, or steel.
Diet preferences: beef, chicken, pork, game, or veal,
vegetarian (this last within reason),
or maidens in or out of season.

Our payment plan is based on need.
We take your house, your soul, your seed.
Please understand:
        a dragon is a work of art.
If you prefer installments, we take your heart.
Just initial your preferred design
and here, on the bottom line . . .
        sign.

THE TOWER BIRD

There was once a king who sat all alone in the top of a high tower room. He saw no one all day long except a tiny golden finch who brought him nuts and seeds and berries out of which the king made a thin, bitter wine.

What magic had brought him to the room, what binding curse kept him there, the king did not know. The curving walls of the tower room, the hard-backed throne, the corbeled window, and the bird were all he knew.

He thought he remembered a time when he had ruled a mighty kingdom; when men had fought at his bidding and women came at his call. Past battles, past loves, were played again and again in his dreams. He found scars on his arms and legs and back to prove them. But his memory had no real door to them, just as the tower room had no real door, only a thin line filled in with bricks.

Each morning the king went to the window that stood head-high in the wall. The window was too small for anything but his voice. He called out, his words spattering into the wind:

· *The Tower Bird* ·

Little bird, little bird,
Come to my hand,
Sing me of my kingdom,
Tell me of my land.

A sudden whirring in the air, and the bird was there, perched on the stone sill.

"O King," the bird began, for it was always formal in its address. "O King, what would you know?"

"Is the land green or sere?" asked the king.

The bird put its head to one side as if considering. It opened its broad little beak several times before answering. "It is in its proper season."

Color suffused the king's face. He was angry with the evasion. He stuttered his second question. "Is . . . is the kingdom at peace or is it at war?" he asked.

"The worm is in the apple," replied the bird, "but the apple is not yet plucked."

The king clutched the arms of his throne. Every day his questions met with the same kinds of answers. Either this was all a test or a jest, a dreaming, or an enchantment too complex for his understanding.

"One more question, O King," said the finch. Under its golden breast a tiny pulse quickened.

The king opened his mouth to speak. "Is . . . is . . ." No more words came out. He felt something cracking inside, as if, with his heart, his whole world were breaking.

The little bird watched a fissure open beneath the king's throne. It grew wider, quickly including the king himself. Without a sound, the king and throne cracked into two uneven pieces. The king was torn between his legs and across the right side of his face. From within the broken parts a smell of soured wine arose.

The bird flew down. It pulled a single white hair from the king's mustache, hovered a moment, then winged out of the window. Round and round the kingdom it flew, looking for a place to nest, a place to build another tower and lay another egg. Perhaps the king that grew from the next egg would be a more solid piece of work.

THE GOLDEN STAIR

i *cut my hair last week;*
all that long gold gone
in a single silent scissoring
after the king was buried.
My husband,
the new king,
wept when he saw it.
But he agreed
that with all I have to do—
the royal tea parties,
the ribbon-cuttings,
the hospital visits,
the endless trips
to factories,
football games,
day care centers—
a short bob is best.

· The Faery Flag ·

It has been months
since he has noticed my hair.
The golden stair *he called it.*
It has been years since the tower.
Now that he is king
we cannot risk another fall,
at least until our sons are grown,
at least until
they have taken over the kingdom.

THE FACE
IN THE CLOTH

There were once a king and queen so in love with one another that they could not bear to be parted, even for a day. To seal their bond, they desperately wanted a child. The king had even made a cradle of oak for the babe with his own hands and placed it by their great canopied bed. But year in and year out, the cradle stood empty.

At last one night, when the king was fast asleep, the queen left their bed. She cast one long, lingering glance at her husband, then, disguising herself with a shawl around her head, she crept out of the castle, for the first time alone. She was bound for a nearby forest where she had heard that three witch-sisters lived. The queen had been told that they might give her what she most desired by taking from her what she least desired to give.

"But I have so much," she thought as she ran through the woods. "Gold and jewels beyond counting. Even the diamond that the king himself put on my hand and from which I would hate to be parted. But though it is probably what I would least desire to give, I would give it gladly in order to have a child.''

The witches' hut squatted in the middle of the wood, and through its window the queen saw the three old sisters sitting by the fire, chanting a spell as soft as a cradle song:

> *Needle and scissors,*
> *Scissors and pins,*
> *Where one life ends,*
> *Another begins.*

And suiting their actions to the words, the three snipped and sewed, snipped and sewed with the invisible thread over and over and over again.

The night was so dark and the three slouching sisters so strange that the queen was quite terrified. But her need was even greater than her fear. She scratched upon the window, and the three looked up from their work.

"Come in," they called out in a single voice.

So she had to go, pulled into the hut by that invisible thread.

"What do you want, my dear?" said the first old sister to the queen through the pins she held in her mouth.

"I want a child," said the queen.

"When do you want it?" asked the second sister, who held a needle high above her head.

"As soon as I can get it," said the queen, more boldly now.

"And what will you give for it?" asked the third, snipping her scissors ominously.

"Whatever is needed," replied the queen. Nervously she turned the ring with the diamond around her finger.

The three witches smiled at one another. Then they each held up a hand with the thumb and forefinger touching in a circle.

"Go," they said. "It is done. All we ask is to be at the birthing to sew the swaddling clothes."

The queen stood still as stone, a river of feeling washing around her. She had been prepared to gift them a fortune. What they asked was so simple, she agreed at once. Then she turned and ran out of the hut all the way to the castle. She never looked back.

Less than a year later, the queen was brought to childbed. But in her great joy, she forgot to mention to the king her promise to the witches. And then in great pain, and because it had been such a small promise after all, she forgot it altogether.

As the queen lay in labor in her canopied bed, there came a knock on the castle door. When the guards opened it, who should be standing there but three slouching old women.

"We have come to be with the queen," said the one with pins in her mouth.

The guards shook their heads.

"The queen promised we could make the swaddling cloth," said the second, holding her needle high over her head.

"We must be by her side," said the third, snapping her scissors.

One guard was sent to tell the king.

The king came to the castle door, his face red with anger, his brow wreathed with sweat.

"The queen told me of no such promise," he said. "And she tells me everything. What possesses you to bother a man at a time like this? Begone." He dismissed them with a wave of his hand.

But before the guards could shut the door upon the ancient sisters, the one with the scissors called out, "Beware, oh King, of promises given." Then all three chanted:

> *Needle and scissors,*
> *Scissors and pins,*
> *Where one life ends,*
> *Another begins.*

The second old woman put her hands above her head and made a circle with her forefinger and thumb. But the one with the pins in her mouth thrust a piece of cloth into the king's hand.

"It is for the babe," she said. "Because of the queen's desire."

Then the three left the castle and were not seen there again.

The king started to look down at the cloth, but there came a loud cry from the bedchamber. He ran back along the corridors, and when he entered the bedroom door, the doctor turned around, a newborn child, still red with birth blood, in his hands.

"It is a girl, Sire," he said.

There was a murmur of praise from the attending women.

The king put out his hands to receive the child and, for the first time, really noticed the cloth he was holding. It was pure white, edged with lace. As he looked at it, his wife's likeness began to appear on it slowly, as if being stitched in with a crimson thread. First the eyes he so loved; then the elegant nose; the soft, full mouth; the dimpled chin.

The king was about to remark on it when the midwife cried out, "It is the queen, Sire. She is dead." And at the same moment, the doctor put the child into his hands.

*   *   *

The royal funeral and the royal christening were held on the same day, and no one in the kingdom knew whether to laugh or cry except the babe, who did both.

Since the king could not bear to part with his wife entirely, he had the cloth with her likeness sewed into the baby's cloak so that wherever she went, the princess carried her mother's face.

As she outgrew one cloak, the white lace was cut away from the old and sewn into the new. And in this way the princess was never without the panel bearing her mother's portrait, nor was she ever allowed to wander far from her father's watchful eyes. Her life was measured by the size of the cloaks which were cut bigger each year, and the likeness of her mother, which seemed to get bigger as well.

The princess grew taller, but she did not grow stronger. She was like a pale copy of her mother. There was never a time that the bloom of health sat on her cheeks. She remained the color of skimmed milk, the color of ocean foam, the color of second-day snow. She was always cold, sitting huddled for warmth inside her picture cloak even on the hottest days, and nothing could part her from it.

The king despaired of his daughter's health, but neither the royal physicians nor philosophers could help. He turned to necromancers and stargazers, to herbalists and diviners. They pushed and prodded and prayed over the princess. They examined the soles of her feet and the movement of her stars. But still she sat cold and whey-colored, wrapped in her cloak.

At last one night, when everyone was fast asleep, the king left his bed and crept out of the castle alone. He had heard that there were three witch sisters who lived nearby who might give him what he most desired by taking from him what he least desired to give. Having lost his queen, he knew there was nothing else he would hate losing—not his fortune, his kingdom, or his throne. He would give it all up gladly to see his daughter, who was his wife's pale reflection, sing and dance and run.

The witches' hut squatted in the middle of the wood, and through its window the king saw the three old sisters. He did not recognize them, but they knew him at once.

"Come in, come in," they called out, though he had not knocked. And he was drawn into the hut as if pulled by an invisible thread.

"We know what you want," said the first.

"We can give you what you desire," said the second.

"By taking what you least wish to give," said the third.

"I have already lost my queen," he said. "So anything else I have is yours so long as my daughter is granted a measure of health." And he started to twist off the ring he wore on his third finger, the ring his wife had been pledged with, to give to the three sisters to seal his part of the bargain.

"Then you must give us—your daughter," said the three.

The king was stunned. For a moment the only sound in the hut was the crackle of fire in the hearth.

"*Never!*" he thundered at last. "What you ask is impossible."

"What *you* ask is impossible," said the first old woman. "Nonetheless, we promise it will be so." She stood. "But if your daughter does not come to us, her life will be worth no more than this." She took a pin from her mouth and held it up. It caught the firelight for a moment. Only a moment.

The king stared. "I know you," he said slowly. "I have seen you before."

The second sister nodded. "Our lives have been sewn together by a queen's desire," she said. She pulled the needle through a piece of cloth she was holding and drew the thread through in a slow, measured stitch.

The third sister began to chant, and at each beat her scissors snapped together:

> *Needle and scissors,*
> *Scissors and pins,*
> *Where one life ends,*
> *Another begins.*

The king cursed them thoroughly, his words hoarse as a rote of war, and left. But partway through the forest, he thought of his daughter like a waning moon asleep in her bed, and wept.

For days he raged in the palace, and his courtiers felt his tongue as painfully as if it were a whip. Even his daughter, usually silent in her shroudlike cloak, cried out.

"Father," she said, "your anger unravels the kingdom, pulling at its loosest threads. What is it? What can I do?" As she spoke, she pulled the cloak more firmly about her shoulders, and the king could swear that the portrait of his wife moved, the lips opening and closing as if the image spoke as well.

The king shook his head and put his hands to his face. "You are all I have left of her," he mumbled. "And now I must let you go."

The princess did not understand, but she put her small faded hands on his. "You must do what you must do, my father," she said.

And though he did not quite understand the why of it, the king brought his daughter into the wood the next night after dark. Setting her on his horse and holding the bridle himself, he led her along the path to the hut of the three crones.

At the door he kissed her once on each cheek and then tenderly kissed the image on her cloak. Then, mounting his horse, he galloped away without once looking back.

Behind him the briars closed over the path, and the forest was still.

Once her father had left, the princess looked around the dark clearing. When no one came to fetch her, she knocked upon the door of the little hut. Getting no answer, she pushed the door open and went in.

The hut was empty, though a fire burned merrily in the hearth. The table was set, and beside the wooden plate were three objects: a needle, a pair of scissors, and a pin. On the hearth wall, engraved in the stone, was a poem. The princess went over to the fire to read it:

> *Needle and scissors,*
> *Scissors and pins,*
> *Where one life ends,*
> *Another begins.*

"How strange," thought the princess, shivering inside her cloak. She looked around the little hut, found a bed with a wooden headboard shaped like a loom, lay down upon the bed and, pulling the cloak around her even more tightly, slept.

In the morning when the princess woke, she was still alone, but there was food on the table, steaming hot. She rose and made a feeble toilette, for there were no mirrors on the wall, and ate the food. All the while she toyed with the needle, scissors, and pin by her plate. She longed for her father and the familiarity of the court, but her father had left her at the hut, and being an obedient child, she stayed.

As she finished her meal, the hearthfire went out, and soon the hut grew chilly. So the princess went outside and sat on a wooden bench by the door. Sunlight illuminated the clearing and wrapped around her shoulders like a golden cloak. Alternately she dozed and woke and dozed again until it grew dark.

When she went inside the hut, the table was once more set with food, and this time she ate eagerly, then went to sleep, dreaming of the needle and scissors and pin. In her dream they danced away from her, refusing to bow when she bade them.

She woke to a cold dawn. The meal was ready, and the smell of it, threading through the hut, got her up. She wondered briefly what hands had done all the work, but, being a princess and used to being served, she did not wonder about it very long.

When she went outside to sit in the sun, she sang snatches of old songs to keep herself company. The sound of her own voice, tentative and slightly off-key, was like an old friend. The tune kept running around and around in her head, and though she did not know where she had heard it before, it fitted perfectly the words carved over the hearth:

Needle and scissors,
Scissors and pins,
Where one life ends,
Another begins.

"This is certainly true," she told herself, "for my life here in the forest is different from my life in the castle, though I myself do not feel changed." And she shivered and pulled the cloak around her.

Several times she stood and walked about the clearing, looking for the path that led out. But it was gone. The brambles were laced firmly together like stitches on a quilt, and when she put a hand to them, a thorn pierced her palm and the blood dripped down onto her cloak, spotting the portrait of her mother and making it look as if she were crying red tears.

It was then the princess knew that she had been abandoned to the magic in the forest. She wondered that she was not more afraid, and tried out different emotions: first fear, then bewilderment, then loneliness; but none of them seemed quite real to her. What she felt, she decided at last, was a kind of lightness, a giddiness, as if she had lost her center, as if she were a balloon, untethered and ready—at last—to let go.

"What a goose I have become," she said aloud. "One or two days without the prattle of courtiers, and I am talking to myself."

But her own voice was a comfort, and she smiled. Then, settling her cloak more firmly about her shoulders, she went back to the hut.

She counted the meager furnishings of the hut as if she were telling beads on a string: door, window, hearth, table, chair, bed. "I wish there were something to *do*," she thought to herself. And as she turned around, the needle on the table was glowing as if a bit of fire had caught in its eye.

She went over to the table and picked up the needle, scissors, and pin and carried them to the hearth. Spreading her cloak on the stones, though careful to keep her mother's image facing up, she sat.

"If I just had some thread," she thought.

Just then she noticed the panel with her mother's portrait. For the first time it seemed small and crowded, spotted from the years. The curls were old-fashioned and overwrought, the mouth a little slack, the chin a touch weak.

"Perhaps if I could borrow a bit of thread from this embroidery," she whispered, "just a bit where it will not be noticed. As I am alone, no one will know but me."

Slowly she began to pick out the crimson thread along one of the tiny curls. She heard a deep sigh as she started, as if it came from the cloak, then realized it had been her own breath that had made the sound. She wound up the thread around the pin until she had quite a lot of it. Then she snipped off the end, knotted it, threaded the needle—and stopped.

"What am I to sew upon?" she wondered. All she had was what she wore. Still, as she had a great need to keep herself busy and nothing else to do, she decided to embroider designs along the edges of her cloak. So she began with what she knew. On the gray panels she sewed a picture of her own castle. It was so real, it seemed as if its banners fluttered in a westerly wind. And as it grew, turret by turret, she began to feel a little warmer, a little more at home.

She worked until it was time to eat, but as she had been in the hut all the while, no magical servants had set the table. So she hunted around the cupboards herself until she found bread and cheese and a pitcher of milk. Making herself a scanty meal, she cleaned away the dishes, then lay down on the bed and was soon asleep.

In the morning she was up with the dawn. She cut herself some bread, poured some milk, and took the meal outside, where she continued to sew. She gave the castle lancet windows, a Lady chapel, cows grazing in the outlying fields, and a moat in which golden carp swam about, their fins stroking the water and making little waves that moved beneath her hand.

When the first bit of thread was used up, she picked out another section of the portrait, all of the curls and a part of the chin. With that thread she embroidered a forest around the castle, where brachet hounds, noses to the ground, sought a scent; a deer started; and a fox lay hidden in a rambling thicket, its ears twitching as the dogs coursed by. She could almost remark their baying, now near, now far away. Then, in the middle of the forest—with a third piece of thread—the princess sewed the hut. Beneath the hut, as she sewed, letters appeared though she did not touch them.

> *Needle and scissors,*
> *Scissors and pins,*
> *Where one life ends,*
> *Another begins.*

She said the words aloud, and as she spoke, puffs of smoke appeared above the embroidered chimney in the hut. It reminded her that it was time to eat.

Stretching, she stood and went into the little house. The bread was gone. She searched the cupboards and could find no more, but there was flour and salt, and so she made herself some flat cakes that she baked in an oven set into the stone of the fireplace. She knew that the smoke from her baking was sending soft clouds above the hut.

While the bread baked and the sweet smell embroidered the air, the princess went back outside. She unraveled more threads from her mother's image: the nose, the mouth, the startled eyes. And with that thread she traced a winding path from the crimson castle with the fluttering banners to the crimson hut with the crown of smoke.

As she sewed, it seemed to her that she could hear the sound of birds—the rapid flutings of a thrush and the jug-jug-jug of a nightingale—and that they came not from the real forest around her but from the cloak. Then she heard, from the very heart of her lap work, the deep, brassy voice of a hunting horn summoning her home.

Looking up from her work, she saw that the brambles around the hut were beginning to part and there was a path heading north toward the castle.

She jumped up, tumbling needle and scissors and pin to the ground, and took a step toward the beckoning path. Then she stopped. The smell of fresh bread stayed her. The embroidery was not yet done. She knew that she had to sew her own portrait onto the white laced panel of the cloak: a girl with crimson cheeks and hair tumbled to her shoulders, walking the path alone. She had to use up the rest of her mother's thread before she was free.

Turning back toward the hut, she saw three old women standing in the doorway, their faces familiar. They smiled and nodded to her, holding out their hands.

The first old woman had the needle and pin nestled in her palm. The second held the scissors by the blades, handles offered. The third old woman shook out the cloak, and as she did so, a breeze stirred the trees in the clearing.

The princess smiled back at them. She held out her hands to receive their gifts. When she was done with the embroidery, though it was hard to part with it, she would give them the cloak. She knew that once it was given, she could go.

BEAUTY AND THE BEAST:
AN ANNIVERSARY

It is winter now,
and the roses are blooming again,
their petals bright against the snow.
My father died last April;
my sisters no longer write,
except at the turning of the year,
content with their fine houses
and their grandchildren.
Beast and I
putter in the gardens
and walk slowly on the forest paths.
He is graying
around the muzzle
and I have silver combs
to match my hair.
I have no regrets.
None.

· The Faery Flag ·

Though sometimes I do wonder
what sounds children
might have made
running across the marble halls,
swinging from the birches
over the roses
in the snow.

HAPPY DENS OR A DAY
IN THE OLD WOLVES' HOME

Nurse Lamb stood in front of the big white house with the black shutters. She shivered. She was a brand-new nurse and this was her very first job.

From inside the house came loud and angry growls. Nurse Lamb looked at the name carved over the door: HAPPY DENS. But it didn't sound like a happy place, she thought, as she listened to the howls from inside.

Shuddering, she knocked on the door.

The only answer was another howl.

Lifting the latch, Nurse Lamb went in.

No sooner had she stepped across the doorstep than a bowl sped by her head. It splattered against the wall. Nurse Lamb ducked, but she was too late. Her fresh white uniform was spotted and dotted with whatever had been in the bowl.

"*Mush!*" shouted an old wolf, shaking his cane at her. "Great howls and thorny paws. I can't stand another day of it. The end of life is nothing but a big bowl of mush."

Nurse Lamb gave a frightened little bleat and turned to go back out the door, but a great big wolf with two black ears and one black paw barred her way. "Mush for breakfast, mush for dinner, and more mush in between," he growled. "That's all they serve us here at Happy Dens, Home for Aging Wolves."

The wolf with the cane added, "When we were young and full of teeth it was never like this." He howled.

Nurse Lamb gave another bleat and ran into the next room. To her surprise it was a kitchen. A large, comfortable-looking pig wearing a white hat was leaning over the stove and stirring an enormous pot. Since the wolves had not followed her in, Nurse Lamb sat down on a kitchen stool and began to cry.

The cook put her spoon down, wiped her trotters with a stained towel, and patted Nurse Lamb on the head, right behind the ears.

"There, there, lambkin," said the cook. "Don't start a new job in tears. We say that in the barnyard all the time."

Nurse Lamb looked up and snuffled. "I . . . I don't think I'm right for this place. I feel as if I have been thrown to the wolves."

The cook nodded wisely. "And, in a manner of speaking, you have been. But these poor old dears are all bark and no bite. Toothless, don't you know. All they can manage is mush."

"But no one told me this was an old *wolves*' home," complained Nurse Lamb. "They just said 'How would you like to work at Happy Dens?' And it sounded like the nicest place in the world."

"And so it is. And so it is," said the cook. "It just takes getting used to."

Nurse Lamb wiped her nose and looked around. "But how could someone like *you* work here? I mean . . ." She dropped her voice to a whisper. "I heard all about it at school. The three little pigs and all. Did you know them?"

The cook sniffed. "And a bad lot they were, too. As we say in the barnyard, 'There's more than one side to every sty.' "

"But I was told that the big bad wolf tried to eat the three little pigs. And he huffed and he puffed and . . ." Nurse Lamb looked confused.

Cook just smiled and began to stir the pot again, lifting up a spoonful to taste.

"And then there was that poor little child in the woods with the red riding hood," said Nurse Lamb. "Bringing the basket of goodies to her sick grandmother."

Cook shook her head and added pepper to the pot. "In the barnyard we say, 'Don't take slop from a kid in a cloak.' " She ladled out a bowlful of mush.

Nurse Lamb stood up. She walked up to the cook and put her hooves on her hips. "But what about that boy Peter. The one who caught the wolf by the tail after he ate the duck. And the hunters came and—"

"Bad press," said a voice from the doorway. It was the wolf with the two black ears. "Much of what you know about wolves is bad press."

Nurse Lamb turned and looked at him. "I don't even know what bad press means," she said.

"It means that only one side of the story has been told. There is another way of telling those very same tales. From the wolf's point of view." He grinned at her. "My name is Wolfgang, and if you will bring a bowl of that thoroughly awful stuff to the table"—he pointed to the pot—"I will tell you *my* side of a familiar tale."

Sheepishly, Nurse Lamb picked up the bowl and followed the wolf into the living room. She put the bowl on the table in front of Wolfgang and sat down. There were half a dozen wolves sitting there.

Nurse Lamb smiled at them timidly.

They smiled back. The cook was right. Only Wolfgang had any teeth. Three, to be exact.

WOLFGANG'S TALE

Once upon a time (began the black-eared wolf) there was a thoroughly nice young wolf. He had two black ears and one black paw. He was a poet and a dreamer.

This thoroughly nice wolf loved to lie about in the woods staring at the lacy curlings of fiddlehead ferns and smelling the wild roses.

He was a vegetarian—except for lizards and an occasional snake, which don't count. He loved carrot cake and was partial to peanut-butter pie.

One day as he lay by the side of a babbling brook, writing a poem that began

> *Twinkle, twinkle, lambkin's eye,*
> *How I wish you were close by . . .*

he heard the sound of a child weeping. He knew it was a human child because only they cry with that snuffling gasp. So the thoroughly nice wolf leaped to his feet and ran over, his hind end waggling, eager to help.

The child looked up from her crying. She was quite young and dressed in a long red riding hood, a lacy dress, white stockings, and black patent-leather Mary Jane shoes. Hardly what you would call your usual hiking-in-the-woods outfit.

"Oh, hello, wolfie," she said. In those days, of course, humans often talked to wolves. "I am quite lost."

The thoroughly nice wolf sat down by her side and held her hand. "There, there," he said. "Tell me where you live."

The child grabbed her hand back. "If I knew that, you silly growler, I wouldn't be lost, would I?"

The thoroughly nice wolf bit back his own sharp answer and asked her in rhyme:

> *Where are you going*
> *My pretty young maid?*
> *Answer me this*
> *And I'll make you a trade.*
>
> *The path through the forest*
> *Is dark and it's long,*
> *So I will go with you*
> *And sing you a song.*

The little girl was charmed. "I'm going to my grandmother's house," she said. "With this." She held up a basket that was covered with a red-checked cloth. The wolf could smell carrot cake. He grinned.

"Oh, poet, what big teeth you have," said the child.

"The better to eat carrot cake with," said the thoroughly nice wolf.

"My granny hates carrot cake," said the child. "In fact, she hates anything but mush."

"What bad taste," said the wolf. "I made up a poem about that once:

If I found someone
Who liked to eat mush,
I'd sit them in front of it,
Then give a . . ."

"*Push!*" shouted the child.

"Why, you're a poet, too," said the wolf.

"I'm really more of a storyteller," said the child, blushing prettily. "But I do love carrot cake."

"All poets do," said the wolf. "So you must be a poet as well."

"Well, my granny is no poet. Every week when I bring the carrot cake over, she dumps it into her mush and mushes it all up together and then makes me eat it with her. She says that I have to learn that life ends with a bowl of mush."

"Great howls!" said the wolf, shuddering. "What a terribly wicked thing to say and do."

"I guess so," said the child.

"Then we must save this wonderful carrot cake from your grandmother," the wolf said, scratching his head below his ears.

The child clapped her hands. "I know," she said. "Let's pretend."

"Pretend?" asked the wolf.

"Let's pretend that you are Granny and I am bringing the cake to *you*. Here, you wear my red riding hood and we'll pretend it's Granny's nightcap and nightgown."

The wolf took her little cape and slung it over his head. He grinned again. He was a poet and he loved pretending.

The child skipped up to him and knocked upon an imaginary door.

The wolf opened it. "Come in. Come in."

"Oh, no," said the child. "My grandmother never gets out of bed."

"Never?" asked the wolf.

"Never," said the child.

"All right," said the thoroughly nice wolf, shaking his head. He lay down on the cool green grass, clasped his paws over his stomach, and made a very loud pretend snore.

The child walked over to his feet and knocked again.

"Who is it?" called out the wolf in a high, weak, scratchy voice.

"It is your granddaughter, Little Red Riding Hood," the child said, giggling.

"Come in, come in. Just lift the latch. I'm in bed with aches and pains and a bad case of the rheumaticks," said the wolf in the high, funny voice.

The child walked in through the pretend door.

"I have brought you a basket of goodies," said the child, putting the basket by the wolf's side. She placed her hands on her hips. "But you know, Grandmother, you look very different today."

"How so?" asked the wolf, opening both his yellow eyes wide.

"Well, Grandmother, what big eyes you have," said the child.

The wolf closed his eyes and opened them again quickly. "The better to see you with, my dear," he said.

"Oh, you silly wolf. She never calls me *dear*. She calls me *Sweetface*. Or *Punkins*. Or her *Airy Fairy Dee*."

"How awful," said the wolf.

"I know," said the child. "But that's what she calls me."

"Well, I can't," said the wolf, turning over on his side. "I'm a poet, after all, and no self-respecting poet could possibly use those words. If I have to call you that, there's no more pretending."

"I guess you can call me *dear*," said the child in a very small voice. "But I didn't know that poets were so particular."

"About *words* we are," said the wolf.

"And you have an awfully big nose," said the child.

The wolf put his paw over his nose. "Now that is uncalled-for," he said. "My nose isn't all that big—for a wolf."

"It's part of the game," said the child.

"Oh, yes, the game. I had forgotten. The better to smell the basket of goodies, my dear," said the wolf.

"And Grandmother, what big teeth you have."

The thoroughly nice wolf sat up. "The better to eat carrot cake with," he said.

At that, the game was over. They shared the carrot cake evenly and licked their fingers, which was not very polite but certainly the best thing to do on a picnic in the woods. And the wolf sang an ode to carrot cake which he made up on the spot:

> *Carrot cake, o carrot cake*
> *The best thing a baker ever could make,*
> *Mushy or munchy*
> *Gushy or crunchy*
> *Eat it by a woodland lake.*

"We are really by a stream," said the child.

"That is what is known as poetic license," said the wolf. "Calling a stream a lake."

"Maybe you can use your license to drive me home."

The wolf nodded. "I will if you tell me your name. I know it's not *really* Little Red Riding Hood."

The child stood up and brushed crumbs off her dress. "It's Elisabet Grimm," she said.

"Of the Grimm family on Forest Lane?" asked the wolf.

"Of course," she answered.

"Everyone knows where that is. I'll take you home right now," said the wolf. He stretched himself from tip to tail. "But what will you tell your mother about her cake?" He took her by the hand.

"Oh, I'm a storyteller," said the child. "I'll think of something."

And she did.

"She did indeed," said Nurse Lamb thoughtfully. She cleared away the now empty bowls and took them back to the kitchen. When she returned, she was carrying a tray full of steaming mugs of coffee.

"I told you I had bad press," said Wolfgang.

"I should say you had," Nurse Lamb replied, passing out the mugs.

"Me, too," said the wolf with the cane.

"You, too, what?" asked Nurse Lamb.

"I had bad press, too, though my story is somewhat different. By the by, my name is Oliver," said the wolf. "Would you like to hear my tale?"

Nurse Lamb sat down. "Oh, please, yes."

OLIVER WOLF'S TALE

Once upon a time there was a very clever young wolf. He had an especially broad, bushy tail and a white star under his chin.

In his playpen he had built tall buildings of blocks and straw.

In the schoolyard he had built forts of mud and sticks.

And once, after a trip with his father to the bricklayer's, he had made a tower of bricks.

Oh, how that clever young wolf loved to build things.

"When I grow up," he said to his mother and father not once but many times, "I want to be an architect."

"That's nice, dear," they would answer, though they wondered about it. After all, no one in their family had ever been anything more than a wolf.

When the clever little wolf was old enough, his father sent him out into the world with a pack of tools and letters from his teachers.

"*This* is a very clever young wolf," read one letter.

"Quite the cleverest I have ever met," said another.

So the clever young wolf set out looking for work.

In a short while he came to a crossroads and who should be there but three punk pigs building themselves houses and making quite a mess of it.

The first little pig was trying to build a house of straw.

"Really," said the clever wolf, "I tried that in the playpen. It won't work. A breath of air will knock it over."

"Well, if you're so clever," said the pig, pushing his sunglasses back up his snout, "why don't you try and blow it down."

The wolf set his pack by the side of the road, rolled up his shirt-sleeves, and huffed and puffed. The house of straw collapsed in a twinkling.

"See," said the clever wolf.

The little pig got a funny look on his face and ran one of his trotters up under his collar.

The wolf turned to the second little pig who had just hammered a nail into the house he was trying to build. It was a makeshift affair of sticks and twigs.

"Yours is not much better, I'm afraid," said the clever wolf.

"Oh, yeah?" replied the pig. "Clever is as clever does." He thumbed his snout at the wolf. "Let's see you blow *this* house down, dog-breath."

The wolf sucked in a big gulp of air. Then he huffed and puffed a bit harder than before. The sticks tumbled down in a heap of dry kindling, just as he knew they would.

The second little pig picked up one of the larger pieces and turned it nervously in his trotters.

"Nyah, nyah nyah, nyah nyah!" said the third little pig, stretching his suspenders and letting them snap back with a loud twang. "Who do you think's afraid of you, little wolf? Try your muzzle on this pile of bricks, hair-face."

"That won't be necessary," said the clever wolf. "Every good builder knows bricks are excellent for houses."

The third little pig sniffed and snapped his suspenders once again.

"However," said the wolf, pointing at the roof, "since you have asked my opinion, I think you missed the point about chimneys. They are supposed to go straight up, not sideways."

"Well, if you're so clever . . ." began the first little pig.

"And have such strong breath . . ." added the second little pig.

"And are such a know-it-all and tell-it-ever . . ." put in the third little pig.

"Why don't you go up there and fix it yourself!" all three said together.

"Well, thank you," said the clever wolf, realizing he had just been given his very first job. "I'll get to it at once." Finding a ladder resting against the side of the brick house, he hoisted his pack of tools onto his back and climbed up onto the roof.

He set the bricks properly, lining them up with his plumb line. He mixed the mortar with care. He was exacting in his measurements and careful in his calculations. The sun was beginning to set before he was done.

"There," he said at last. "That should do it." He expected, at the very least, a thank-you from the pigs. But instead all he got was a loud laugh from the third little pig, a snout-thumbing from the second, and a nasty wink from the first.

The clever wolf shrugged his shoulders. After all, pigs will be pigs and he couldn't expect them to be wolves. But when he went to climb down he found they had removed the ladder.

"Clever your way out of this one, fuzz-ball," shouted the third little pig. Then they ran inside the house, turned up the stereo, and phoned their friends for a party.

The only way down was the chimney. But the wolf had to wait until the bricks and mortar had set as hard as stone. That took half the night. When at last the chimney was ready, the wolf slowly made his way down the inside, his pack on his back.

The pigs and their friends heard him coming. And between one record and the next, they shoved a pot of boiling mush into the hearth. They laughed themselves silly when the wolf fell in.

"That's how things end, fur-tail," the pigs shouted. "With a bowl of mush."

Dripping and unhappy, the wolf ran out the door. He vowed never to associate with pigs again. And to this day—with the exception of the cook—he never has. And being a well-brought-up wolf, as well as clever, he has never told his side of the story until today.

"Well, the pigs sure talked about it," said Nurse Lamb, shaking her head. "They way *they* have told it, it is quite a different story."

"Nobody listens to pigs," said Oliver Wolf. He looked quickly at the kitchen door.

"I'm not so sure," said a wolf who had a patch over his eye. "I'm not so sure."

"So you're not so sure," said Oliver. "Bet you think you're pretty clever, Lone Wolf."

"No," said Lone Wolf. "I never said I was clever. *You* are the clever little wolf."

Wolfgang laughed. "So clever he was outwitted by a pack of punk pigs."

The other wolves laughed.

"You didn't do so well with one human child," answered Oliver.

"Now, now, now," said the cook, poking her head in through the door. "As we say in the barnyard, 'Words are like wood, a handy weapon.' "

"No weapons. No fighting," said Nurse Lamb, standing up and shaking her hoof at the wolves. "We are supposed to be telling stories, not getting into fights."

Lone Wolf stared at her. "I never in my life ran from a fight. Not if it was for a good cause."

Nurse Lamb got up her courage and put her hand on his shoulder. "I believe you," she said. "Why not tell me about some of the good causes you fought for?"

Lone Wolf twitched his ears. "All right," he said at last. "I'm not boasting, you understand. Just setting the record straight."

Nurse Lamb looked over at the kitchen door. The old sow winked at her and went back to work.

LONE WOLF'S TALE

Once upon a time there was a kind, tender, and compassionate young wolf. He had a black patch over one eye and another black patch at the tip of his tail. He loved to help the under-dog, the under-wolf, the under-lamb, and even the under-pig.

His basement was full of the signs of his good fights. Signs like LOVE A TREE and HAVE YOU KISSED A FLOWER TODAY? and PIGS ARE PEOPLE, TOO! and HONK IF YOU LOVE A WEASEL.

One day he was in the basement running off petitions on his mimeo machine when he heard a terrible noise.

KA-BLAAAAAAAM   KA-BLOOOOOOOIE.

It was the sound a gun makes in the forest.

Checking his calendar, the kind and tender wolf saw with horror that it was opening day of duck-hunting season. Quickly he put on his red hat and red vest. Then he grabbed up the signs he had made for that occasion: SOME DUCKS CAN'T DUCK and EAT CORN NOT CORN-EATERS and DUCKS HAVE MOTHERS, TOO. Then he ran out of his door and down the path as fast as he could go.

KA-BLAAAAAAAM   KA-BLOOOOOOOIE.

116

The kind and tender wolf knew just where to go. Deep in the forest was a wonderful pond where the ducks liked to stop on their way north. The food was good, the reeds comfortable, the prices reasonable, and the linens changed daily.

When the kind and tender wolf got to the pond, all he could see was one small and very frightened mallard in the middle of the pond and thirteen hunters around the edge.

"Stop!" he shouted as the hunters raised their guns.

This did not stop them.

The kind and tender wolf tried again, shouting anything he could think of. "We shall overcome," he called. "No smoking. No nukes. Stay off the grass."

Nothing worked. The hunters sighted their guns. The wolf knew it was time to act.

He put one of the signs in the water and sat on it. He picked up another sign as a paddle. Using his tail as a rudder, he pushed off into the pond and rowed toward the duck.

"I will save you," he cried. "We are brothers. Quack."

The mallard looked confused. Then it turned and swam toward the wolf. When it reached him, it climbed onto the sign and quacked back.

"Saved," said the kind and tender wolf triumphantly, neglecting to notice that their combined weight was making the cardboard sign sink. But when the water was up to his chin, the wolf suddenly remembered he could not swim.

"Save yourself, friend," he called out, splashing great waves and swallowing them.

The mallard was kind and tender, too. It pushed the drowning wolf to shore and then, hidden by a patch of reeds, gave the well-meaning wolf beak-to-muzzle resuscitation. Then the bird flew off behind the cover of trees. The hunters never saw it go.

But they found the wolf, his fur all soggy.

"Look!" said one who had his name, *Peter*, stenciled on the pocket of his coat. "There are feathers on this wolf's jaws and in his whiskers. He has eaten *our* duck."

And so the hunters grabbed up the kind and tender wolf by his tail and slung him on top of the remaining sign. They marched him once around the town and threw him into jail for a week, where they gave him nothing to eat but mush.

"Now, wolf," shouted the hunter Peter when they finally let him out of jail, "don't you come back here again or it will be mush for you from now 'til the end of your life."

The kind and tender wolf, nursing his hurt tail and his aching teeth, left town. The next day the newspaper ran a story that read: PETER & THE WOLF FIGHT. PETER RUNS FOR MAYOR. VOWS TO KEEP WOLF FROM DOOR. And to this day no one believes the kind and tender wolf's side of the tale.

"I believe it," said Nurse Lamb looking at Lone Wolf with tears in her eyes. "In fact, I believe all of you." She stood up and collected the empty mugs.

"Hurray!" said the cook, peeking in the doorway. "Maybe this is one young nurse we'll keep."

"Keep?" Nurse Lamb suddenly looked around, all her fear coming back. Lone Wolf was cleaning his nails. Three old wolves had dozed off. Wolfgang was gazing at the ceiling. But Oliver grinned at her and licked his chops. "What do you mean, keep?"

"Do you want *our* side of the story?" asked Oliver, still grinning. "Or the nurses'?"

Nurse Lamb gulped.

Oliver winked.

Then Nurse Lamb knew they were teasing her. "Oh, you big bad wolf," she said and patted him on the head. She walked back into the kitchen.

"You know," she said to the cook. "I think I'm going to like it here. I think I can help make it a real *happy* HAPPY DEN. I'll get them to write down their stories. And maybe we'll make a book of them. Life doesn't *have* to end with a bowl of mush."

Stirring the pot, the cook nodded and smiled.

"In fact," said Nurse Lamb loudly, "why don't we try chicken soup for lunch?"

From the dining room came a great big cheer.

ABOUT THE AUTHOR

Jane Yolen is one of America's most distinguished creators of original tales in the classic tradition, and her works have brought her numerous honors, including the Kerlan Award, the Golden Kite Award, and the World Fantasy Award. Author of more than one hundred books, she writes for both children and adults, and is also an editor, a gifted storyteller, and a folk musician. She is a graduate of Smith College, where she has taught courses in children's literature and creative writing, and she has received an honorary doctorate degree from the College of Our Lady of the Elms. The richness of verbal imagery in her writing has inspired many artists to collaborate with her, and her book *Owl Moon*, illustrated by John Schoenherr, was recently awarded the prestigious Caldecott Medal. Among her outstanding story collections are *Dream Weaver*, *Neptune Rising*, and the enduringly popular *The Girl Who Cried Flowers*, which has been called a modern classic. With her husband and the youngest of their three children, Ms. Yolen lives and writes in a lovely old farmhouse in western Massachusetts.